Published by Sophene 2019

Native American Tales was first published in 2019 by Sophene Pty Ltd.

These tales were originally compiled by
James Mooney and W. T. Larned.

www.sophenebooks.com

ISBN-13: 978-1-925937-17-6

NATIVE AMERICAN TALES

A COLLECTION OF CLASSIC NATIVE AMERICAN FOLK TALES

NATIVE AMERICAN TALES

A COLLECTION OF CLASSIC NATIVE AMERICAN FOLK TALES

CONTENTS

THE CHILD OF THE
EVENING STAR

Once upon a time, on the shores of the great lake, Gitchee Gumee, there lived a hunter who had ten beautiful young daughters. Their hair was dark and glossy as the wings of the blackbird, and when they walked or ran it was with the grace and freedom of the deer in the forest.

Thus it was that many suitors came to court them—brave and handsome young men, straight as arrows, fleet of foot, who could travel from sun to sun without fatigue. They were sons of the prairie, wonderful horsemen who would ride at breakneck speed without saddle or stirrup. They could catch a wild horse with a noose, tame him in a magical way by breathing into his nostrils, then mount him and gallop off as if he always had been ridden. There were those also who came from afar in canoes, across the waters of the Great Lake, canoes which shot swiftly along, urged by the strong, silent sweep of the paddle.

All of them brought presents with which they hoped to gain the father's favor. Feathers from the wings of the eagle who soars high up near the sun; furs of fox and beaver and the thick, curly hair of the bison; beads of many colors, and wampum, the shells which the Indians used for money; the quills of the porcupine and the claws of the grizzly bear; deerskin dressed to such a softness that it crumpled up in the hands—these and many other things they brought.

One by one, the daughters were wooed and married, until nine of them had chosen husbands. One by one, other tents were reared, so that instead of the single family lodge on the shores of the lake there were tents enough to form a little village. For the country was a rich one, and there was game and fish enough for all.

There remained the youngest daughter, Oweenee—the fairest of them all. Gentle as she was beautiful, none was so kind of heart. Unlike her proud and talkative elder sisters, Oweenee was shy and modest, and spoke but little. She loved to wander alone in the woods, with no company but the birds and squirrels and her own thoughts. What these thoughts were we can only guess; from her dreamy eyes and sweet expression, one could but suppose that nothing selfish or mean or hateful ever came into her mind. Yet Oweenee, modest though she was, had a spirit of her own. More than one suitor had found this out. More than one conceited young man, confident that he could win her, went away crestfallen when Oweenee began to laugh at him.

The truth is, Oweenee seemed hard to please. Suitor after suitor came—handsome, tall young men, the handsomest and the bravest in all the country round. Yet this fawn-eyed maiden would have none of them. One was too tall, another too short; one too thin, another too fat. At least, that was the excuse she gave for sending them away. Her proud sisters had little patience with her. It seemed to be questioning their own taste; for Oweenee, had she said the word, might have gained a husband more attractive than any of theirs. Yet no one was good enough. They could not understand her; so they ended by despising her as a silly and unreasonable girl.

Her father, too, who loved her dearly and wished her to be happy, was much puzzled. "Tell me, my daughter," he said to her one day, "Is it your wish never to marry? The handsomest young men in the land have sought you in marriage, and you have sent them all away—often with a poor excuse.

Why is it?"

Oweenee looked at him with her large, dark eyes.

"Father," she said at last. "It is not that I am wilful. But it seems somehow as if I had the power to look into the hearts of men. It is the heart of a man, and not his face, that really matters; and I have not yet found one youth who in this sense is really beautiful."

Soon after, a strange thing happened. There came into the little village an Indian named Osseo, many years older than Oweenee. He was poor and ugly, too. Yet Oweenee married him.

How the tongues of her nine proud sisters did wag! Had the spoiled little thing lost her mind? they asked. Oh, well! They always knew she would come to a bad end; but it was pretty hard on the family.

Of course they could not know what Oweenee had seen at once—that Osseo had a generous nature and a heart of gold; that beneath his outward ugliness was the beauty of a noble mind, and the fire and passion of a poet. That is why Oweenee loved him; knowing, too, that he needed her care, she loved him all the more.

Now, though Oweenee did not suspect it, Osseo was really a beautiful youth on whom an evil spell had been cast. He was in truth the son of the King of the Evening Star—that Evening Star which shines so gloriously in the western sky, just above the rim of the earth, as the sun is setting. Often on a clear evening it hung suspended in the purple twilight like some glittering jewel. So close it seemed, and so friendly, that the little children would reach out their hands, thinking that they might grasp it ere it was swallowed by the night, and keep it always for their own. But the older ones would say: "Surely it must be a bead on the garments of the Great Spirit as he walks in the evening through the garden of the heavens."

Little did they know that the poor, despised Osseo had really descended from that star. And when he, too, stretched out his arms toward it, and murmured words they could not understand, they all made sport of him.

There came a time when a great feast was prepared in a neighboring village, and all of Oweenee's kinsfolk were invited to attend. They set out on foot—the nine proud sisters, with their husbands, walking ahead, much pleased with themselves and their finery, and all chattering like magpies. But Oweenee walked behind in silence, and with her walked Osseo.

The sun had set; in the purple twilight, over the edge of the earth, sparkled the Evening Star. Osseo, pausing, stretched out his hands toward it, as if imploring pity; but when the others saw him in this attitude they all made merry, laughing and joking and making unkind remarks.

"Instead of looking up in the sky," said one of the sisters, "he had better be looking on the ground. Else he may stumble and break his neck." Then calling back to him, she cried: "Look out! Here's a big log. Do you think you can manage to climb over it?"

Osseo made no answer; but when he came to the log he paused again. It was the trunk of a huge oak-tree blown down by the wind. There it had lain for years, just as it fell; and the leaves of many summers lay thick upon it. There was one thing, though, the sisters had not noticed. The tree-trunk was not a solid one, but hollow, and so big around that a man could walk inside it from one end to the other without stooping.

But Osseo did not pause because he was unable to climb

over it. There was something mysterious and magical in the appearance of the great hollow trunk; and he gazed at it a long time, as if he had seen it in a dream, and had been looking for it ever since.

"What is it, Osseo?" asked Oweenee, touching him on the arm. "Do you see something that I cannot see?"

But Osseo only gave a shout that echoed through the forest, and leaped inside the log. Then as Oweenee, a little alarmed, stood there waiting, the figure of a man came out from the other end. Could this be Osseo? Yes, it was he—but how transformed! No longer bent and ugly, no longer weak and ailing; but a beautiful youth—-vigorous and straight and tall. His enchantment was at an end.

But the evil spell had not been wholly lifted, after all. As Osseo approached he saw that a great change was taking place in his loved one. Her glossy black hair was turning white, deep wrinkles lined her face; she walked with a feeble step, leaning on a staff. Though he had regained his youth and beauty, she in turn had suddenly grown old.

"O, my dearest one!" he cried. "The Evening Star has mocked me in letting this misfortune come upon you. Better far had I remained as I was; gladly would I have borne the insults and laughter of your people rather than you should be made to suffer."

"As long as you love me," answered Oweenee, "I am perfectly content. If I had the choice to make, and only one of us could be young and fair, it is you that I would wish to be beautiful."

Then he took her in his arms and caressed her, vowing that he loved her more than ever for her goodness of heart; and together they walked hand in hand, as lovers do.

When the proud sisters saw what had happened they could scarcely believe their eyes. They looked enviously at Osseo, who was now far handsomer than any one of their husbands, and much their superior in every other way. In his eyes was the wonderful light of the Evening Star, and when he spoke all men turned to listen and admire him. But the hard-hearted sisters had no pity for Oweenee. Indeed, it rather pleased them to see that she could no longer dim their beauty, and to realize that people would no longer be singing her praises in their jealous ears.

The feast was spread, and all made merry but Osseo. He sat like one in a dream, neither eating nor drinking. From time to time he would press Oweenee's hand, and speak a word of comfort in her ear. But for the most part he sat there, gazing through the door of the tent at the star-besprinkled sky.

Soon a silence fell on all the company. From out of the night, from the dark, mysterious forest, came the sound of music—a low, sweet music that was like, yet unlike, the song sung by the thrush in summer twilight. It was magical music such as none had ever heard, coming, as it seemed, from a great distance, and rising and falling on the quiet summer evening. All those at the feast wondered as they listened. And well they might! For what to them was only music, was to Osseo a voice that he understood, a voice from the sky itself, the voice of the Evening Star. These were the words that he heard:

"Suffer no more, my son; for the evil spell is broken, and hereafter no magician shall work you harm. Suffer no more; for the time has come when you shall leave the earth and dwell here with me in the heavens. Before you is a dish on which my light has fallen, blessing it and giving it a magic virtue. Eat of this dish, Osseo, and all will be well."

So Osseo tasted the food before him, and behold! The tent began to tremble, and rose slowly into the air; up, up above the tree-tops—up, up toward the stars. As it rose, the things within it were wondrously changed. The kettles of clay became bowls of silver, the wooden dishes were scarlet shells, while the bark of the roof and the poles supporting it were transformed into some glittering substance that sparkled in the rays of the stars. Higher and higher it rose. Then the nine proud sisters and their husbands were all changed into birds. The men became robins, thrushes and woodpeckers. The sisters were changed into various birds with bright plumage; the four who had chattered most, whose tongues were always wagging, now appeared in the feathers of the magpie and bluejay.

Osseo sat gazing at Oweenee. Would she, too, change into a bird, and be lost to him? The very thought of it made him bow his head with grief; then, as he looked at her once more, he saw her beauty suddenly restored, while the color of her garments was the color only to be found where the dyes of the rainbow are made.

Again the tent swayed and trembled as the currents of the air bore it higher and higher, into and above the clouds; up, up, up—till at last it settled gently on the land of the Evening Star.

Osseo and Oweenee caught all the birds, and put them in a great silver cage, where they seemed quite content in each other's company. Scarcely was this done when Osseo's father, the King of the Evening Star, came to greet them. He was attired in a flowing robe, spun from star-dust, and his long white hair hung like a cloud upon his shoulders.

"Welcome," he said, "my dear children. Welcome to the

kingdom in the sky that has always awaited you. The trials you have passed through have been bitter; but you have borne them bravely, and now you will be rewarded for all your courage and devotion. Here you will live happily; yet of one thing you must beware."

He pointed to a little star in the distance—a little, winking star, hidden from time to time by a cloud of vapor.

"On that star," he continued, "lives a magician named Wabeno. He has the power to dart his rays, like so many arrows, at those he wishes to injure. He has always been my enemy; it was he who changed Osseo into an old man and cast him down upon the earth. Have a care that his light does not fall upon you. Luckily, his power for evil has been greatly weakened; for the friendly clouds have come to my assistance, and form a screen of vapor through which his arrows cannot penetrate." The happy pair fell upon their knees, and kissed his hands in gratitude.

"But these birds," said Osseo, rising and pointing to the cage. "Is this also the work of Wabeno, the magician?"

"No," answered the King of the Evening Star. "It was my own power, the power of love, that caused your tent to rise and bear you hither. It was likewise by my power that the envious sisters and their husbands were transformed into birds. Because they hated you and mocked you, and were cruel and scornful to the weak and the old, I have done this thing. It is not so great a punishment as they deserve. Here in the silver cage they will be happy enough, proud of their handsome plumage, strutting and twittering to their hearts' content. Hang the cage there, at the doorway of my dwelling. They shall be well cared for."

Thus it was that Osseo and Oweenee came to live in the

kingdom of the Evening Star; and, as the years passed by, the little winking star where Wabeno, the magician, lived grew pale and paler and dim and dimmer, till it quite lost its power to harm. Meanwhile a little son had come to make their happiness more perfect, a charming boy with the dark, dreamy eyes of his mother and the strength and courage of Osseo.

It was a wonderful place for a little boy to live in—close to the stars and the moon, with the sky so near that it seemed a kind of curtain for his bed, and all the glory of the heavens spread out before him. But sometimes he was lonely, and wondered what the Earth was like—the Earth his father and mother had come from. He could see it far, far below— so far that it looked no bigger than an orange; and sometimes he would stretch out his hands toward it, just as the little children on earth stretch out their hands for the moon.

His father had made him a bow, with little arrows, and this was a great delight to him. But still he was lonely, and wondered what the little boys and girls on earth were doing, and whether they would be nice to play with. The Earth must be a pretty place, he thought, with so many people living on it. His mother had told him strange stories of that far-away land, with its lovely lakes and rivers, its great, green forests where the deer and the squirrel lived, and the yellow, rolling prairies swarming with buffalo.

These birds, too, in the great silver cage had come from the Earth, he was told; and there were thousands and thousands just like them, as well as others even more beautiful that he had never seen at all. Swans with long, curved necks, that floated gracefully on the waters; whip-poor-wills that called at night from the woods; the robin redbreast, the dove and the swallow. What wonderful birds they must be!

Sometimes he would sit near the cage, trying to understand the language of the feathered creatures inside. One day a strange idea came into his head. He would open the door of the cage and let them out. Then they would fly back to Earth, and perhaps they would take him with them. When his father and mother missed him they would be sure to follow him to the Earth, and then—

He could not quite see just how it would all end. But he found himself quite close to the cage, and the first thing he knew he had opened the door and let out all the birds. Round and round they flew; and now he was half sorry, and a little afraid as well. If the birds flew back to Earth, and left him there, what would his grandfather say?

"Come back, come back!" he called.

But the birds only flew around him in circles, and paid no attention to him. At any moment they might be winging their way to the Earth.

"Come back, I tell you!" he cried, stamping his foot and waving his little bow. "Come back, I say, or I'll shoot you."

Then, as they would not obey him, he fitted an arrow to his bow and let it fly. So well did he aim that the arrow sped through the plumage of a bird, and the feathers fell all around. The bird itself, a little stunned but not much hurt, fell down; and a tiny trickle of blood stained the ground where it lay. But it was no longer a bird, with an arrow in its wing; instead, there stood in its place a beautiful young woman.

Now, no one who lives in the stars is ever permitted to shed blood, whether it be of man, beast or bird. So when the few drops fell upon the Evening Star, everything was changed. The boy suddenly found himself sinking slowly downward, held up by invisible hands, yet ever sinking closer and closer to the Earth. Soon he could see its green hills and the swans floating on the water, till at last he rested on a grassy island in a great lake. Lying there, and looking up at the sky, he could see the tent descending, too. Down it softly drifted, till it in turn sank upon the island; and in it were his father and mother, Osseo and Oweenee—returned to earth, to live once more among men and women and teach them how to live. For they had learned many things in their life upon the Evening Star; and the children of Earth would be better for the knowledge.

As they stood there, hand in hand, all the enchanted birds came fluttering after, falling and fluttering through the air. Then as each one touched the Earth, it was no longer a bird they saw, but a human being. A human being, yet not quite as before; for now they were only dwarfs, Little People, or Pygmies; Puk-Wudjies, as the Indians called them. Happy Little People they became, seen only by a few. Fishermen, they say, would sometimes get a glimpse of them—dancing in the light of the Evening Star, of a summer night, on the sandy, level beach of the Great Lake.

IAGOO, THE STORY-TELLER

There never was anyone so wise and knowing as old Iagoo. There never was an Indian who saw and heard so much. He knew the secrets of the woods and fields, and understood the language of birds and beasts. All his life long he had lived out of doors, wandering far in the forest where the wild deer hide, or skimming the waters of the lake in his birch-bark canoe.

Besides the things he had learned for himself, Iagoo knew much more. He knew the fairy tales and the wonder stories told him by his grandfather, who had heard them from his grandfather, and so on, away back to the time when the world was young and strange, and there was magic in almost everything.

Iagoo was a great favorite with the children. No one knew better where to find the beautiful, colored shells which he strung into necklaces for the little girls. No one could teach them so well just where to look for the grasses which their nimble fingers wove into baskets. For the boys he made bows and arrows—bows from the ash-tree, that would bend far back without breaking, and arrows, strong and straight, from the sturdy oak.

But most of all, Iagoo won the children's hearts with his stories. Where did the robin get his red breast? How did fire find its way into the wood, so that an Indian can get it out again by rubbing two sticks together? Why was Coyote, the prairie wolf, so much cleverer than the other animals; and why was he always looking behind him when he ran? It was old Iagoo who could tell you where and why.

Now, winter was the time for story-telling. When the

snow lay deep on the ground, the North. Wind came howling from his home in the Land of Ice, and the cold moon shone from the frosty sky, it was then that the Indians gathered in the wigwam. It was then that Iagoo sat by the fire of blazing logs, and the little boys and girls gathered around him.

"Whoo, whoo!" wailed the North Wind. The sparks leapt up, and Iagoo laid another log on the fire. "Whoo, whoo!" What a mischievous old fellow was this North Wind! One could almost see him—his flowing hair all hung with icicles. If the wigwam were not so strong he would blow it down, and if the fire were not so bright he would put it out. But the wigwam was made on purpose, for just such a time as this; and the forest nearby had logs to last forever. So the North Wind could only gnash his teeth, and say, "Whoo, whoo!"

One little girl, more timid than the rest, would draw nearer and put her hand on the old man's arm. "O, Iagoo," she said, "Just listen! Do you think he can hurt us?"

"Have no fear," answered Iagoo. "The North Wind can do no harm to anyone who is brave and cheerful. He blusters, and makes a lot of noise; but at heart he is really a big coward, and the fire will soon frighten him away. Suppose I tell you a story about it."

And the story Iagoo told we shall now tell to you, the story of how Shin-ge-bis fooled the North Wind.

THE LITTLE BOY AND GIRL IN THE CLOUDS

Iagoo, the Story-Teller, was seated one evening in his favorite corner, gazing into the embers of the log fire like one in a dream.

At such a time the children knew better than to interrupt him by asking questions or teasing him for a story. They knew that Iagoo was turning over in his mind the strange things he had heard and the wonderful things he had seen; that the burning logs and red coals took on curious shapes and made odd pictures that only he could understand, and that if they did not disturb him he would presently begin to speak.

On this particular evening, however, though they waited patiently and talked to one another only in low whispers, Iagoo kept on sitting there as if he were made of stone. They began to fear that he had forgotten them, and that bed-time would come without a story. So at last little Morning Glory, who was always asking questions, thought of one she had never asked before.

"Iagoo!" she said; and then she stopped, fearing to offend him.

At the sound of her voice the old man roused himself, as if his mind had been away on a long journey into the past.

"What is it, Morning Glory?"

"Iagoo—can you tell me—were the mountains always here?"

The old man looked at her gravely. No matter how hard the question was, or how unexpected, Iagoo was always glad to answer. He never said: "I'm too busy, don't bother me," or, "Wait till some other time." So when Morning Glory asked him this very peculiar question, he nodded his wise old head, saying:

"Do you know, I've often asked myself that very thing: Were the mountains always here?"

He paused, and looked once more into the fire, as if the answer was to be found there if he only looked long enough. At last he spoke again:

"Yes, I think it must be true that the mountains were always here—the mountains and the hills. They were made when the world was made—a long, long time ago; and the story of how the world was made you have heard before. But there is one high hill that was not always here—a hill that grew like magic, all of a sudden. Did I ever tell you the story of the Big Rock—how it rose and rose, and carried the little boy and girl up among the clouds?"

"No, no!" shouted the children in a chorus. "You never told us that one. Tell it to us now."

And this is the story of the magical Big Rock, as old Iagoo heard it from his grandfather, who heard it from his great-grandfather, who was almost old enough to have been there himself when it all happened:

In the days when all animals and men lived on friendly terms, when Coyote, the prairie wolf, was not a bad sort of fellow when you came to know him, and even the Mountain Lion would growl pleasantly and pass you the time of day—there lived in a beautiful valley a little boy and girl.

This valley was a lovely place to live in; never was such a playground anywhere on earth. It was like a great green carpet stretching for miles and miles, and when the wind blew upon the long grass it was like looking at the waves of the sea. Flowers of all colors bloomed in the beautiful valley, berries grew thick on the bushes, and birds filled the summer air with their songs.

Best of all, there was nothing whatever to fear.

Never was such a play-ground anywhere. The children could wander at will—watching the gay butterflies, making friends with the squirrels and rabbits, or following the flight of the bee to some tree where his honey is stored.

As for the wild animals, it was all very different from what it is to-day, when they keep the poor things in cages, or coop them up in a little patch of ground behind a high fence. In the beautiful valley the animals ran free and happily, as they were meant to do. The Bear was a big, lazy, good-natured fellow, who lived on berries and wild honey in the summer, and in winter crept into his cavern in the rocks and slept there till the spring. The deer were not only gentle, but tame as sheep, and often came to crop the tender grass that grew where the two children were accustomed to play.

They loved all the animals, and the animals loved them; but perhaps their special favorites were Jack Rabbit and Antelope. Jack Rabbit had long legs, and long ears—almost as long as a mule's, and no animal of his size could jump so high. But of course he could not jump as high as Antelope—the name of a beautiful little deer, with short horns and slender legs, who could run like the wind.

Another thing that made the happy valley such a pleasant place to live in was the river that flowed through it. All the animals came from miles around to drink from its clear, cool waters, and to bathe in it on a hot summer day. One shallow pool seemed made especially for the little boy and girl. Their friend, the Beaver, with his flat tail like an oar and his feet webbed like a duck's, had taught them how to swim almost as soon as they had learned to walk; and to splash around in the pool on a warm afternoon was among their greatest pleasures.

One day in mid-summer the water was so pleasant that they remained in the pool much longer than usual, so that when at last they came out they were quite tired. And as they were a little chilled besides, they looked around for a good place where they could get dry and warm.

"Let's climb up on that big, flat rock, with the moss on it," said the little boy. "We've never done it before. It would be lots of fun."

So he clambered up the side of the rock, which was only a few feet high, and drew his sister up after him. Then they lay down to rest, and pretty soon, without intending it at all, they were fast asleep.

Nobody knows how it happened that exactly at this time the rock began to rise and grow. But it did happen, because there it is today, high and bare and steep, higher than the other hills in the valley. As the children slept, it rose and rose, inch by inch, foot by foot; by the next day it was taller than the tallest trees.

Meanwhile their father and mother were searching for them everywhere, but all in vain; nor was any trace of them to be found. No one had seen them climb up on the rock, and everyone concerned was too much excited to notice what had really happened to it. The parents wandered far and wide saying: "Antelope, have you seen our little boy and girl? Jack Rabbit, you must have seen our little boy and girl." But none of the animals had seen them.

At last they met Coyote, the cleverest of them all, trotting along the valley with his nose in the air; so they put the same question to him.

"No," said Coyote. "I have not seen them for a long time. But my nose was given me to smell with, and my brains were given me to think with. So who can tell but that I may help you?"

He trotted by their side, along the banks of the river, and pretty soon they came to the pool where the children had been in swimming. Coyote sniffed and sniffed. He ran around and around, with his nose to the ground; then he ran right up to the rock, put his forepaws up as high as he could reach, and sniffed again.

"H-m-m!" he grunted. "I cannot fly like the Eagle, and I cannot swim like the Beaver. But neither am I stupid like the Bear, nor ignorant like the Jack Rabbit. My nose has never deceived me yet; your little boy and girl must be up there on that rock."

"But how could they get there?" asked the astonished parents. For the rock was now so high that the top was lost to sight in the clouds.

"That is not the question," said Coyote severely, unwilling to admit there was anything he did not know. "That is not the question at all. Anybody could ask that. The only question worth asking is: How are we to get them down again?"

So they called all the animals together, to talk it over and see what could be done. Then the Bear said: "If I could only put my arms around the rock I could climb it. But it is much too big for that." And the Fox said: "If it were only a deep hole, instead of a high hill, I would be able to help you." And the Beaver said: "If it were just a place out in the water I could swim to, I'd show you very quickly."

But as this kind of talk did not take them very far, they decided to try what jumping would do. There seemed to be no other way; and as each one was anxious to do his part, the smallest one was permitted to make the first attempt. So the Mouse made a funny little hop, about as high as your hand. The Squirrel went a little higher. Jack Rabbit made the highest jump of his life, and almost broke his back, to no purpose. Antelope gave a great bound in the air, but managed to light on his feet again without doing himself any harm. Finally, the Mountain Lion went a long way off, to get a good start, ran toward the rock with great leaps, sprang straight up—and fell and rolled over on his back. He had made a higher jump than any of them; but it was not nearly high enough.

No one knew what to do next. It seemed as if the little boy and girl must be left sleeping on forever, up among the clouds. Suddenly they heard a tiny voice saying:

"Perhaps if you let *me* try, I might *climb* up the rock." They all looked around in surprise, wondering who it was that spoke; and at first they could see nobody, and thought that Coyote must be playing a trick on them. But Coyote was as much surprised as anyone.

"Wait a minute. I'm coming as fast as I can," said the tiny voice again. Then a Measuring Worm crawled out of the grass—a funny little worm that made its way along by hunching up its back and drawing itself ahead an inch at a time.

"Ho, ho!" said the Mountain Lion, from deep down in his throat. He always spoke that way when his dignity was offended. "Ho, ho! Did you ever hear of such impudence? If I, a lion, have failed, how can a miserable little crawling worm like you hope to succeed; just tell me that!"

"It's downright silly," said Jack Rabbit. "That's what it is. I never heard of such conceit."

However, after much talk, they agreed at last that it could

do no harm to let him try. So the Measuring Worm made his way slowly to the rock, and began to climb. In a few minutes he was higher than Jack Rabbit had jumped. Soon he was farther up than the lion had been able to leap: before long he had climbed out of sight.

It took the Measuring Worm a whole month, climbing day and night, to reach the top of the magic rock. When he got there he awakened the little boy and girl, who were much surprised to see where they were, and guided them safely down along a path no one else knew anything about. Thus, by patience and perseverance, the weak little creature was able to do something that the Bear, for all his size, and the Lion, for all his strength, could never have done at all. That was a long time ago; today there are no more lions or bears in the valley, and no one ever thinks of them. But everybody thinks of the Measuring Worm, because the Big Rock is still there, and the Indians have named it after him. Tu-tok-a-nu-la, they call it, a big name indeed for a little fellow, yet by no means too big when you come to think of the big, brave thing he did.

SHIN-GE-BIS FOOLS THE NORTH WIND

Long, long ago, in the time when only a few people lived upon the earth, there dwelt in the North a tribe of fishermen. Now, the best fish were to be found in the summer season, far up in the frozen places where no one could live in the winter at all. For the King of this Land of Ice was a fierce old man called Ka-bib-on-okka by the Indians—meaning in our language, the North Wind.

Though the Land of Ice stretched across the top of the world for thousands and thousands of miles, Ka-bib-on-okka was not satisfied. If he could have had his way there would have been no grass or green trees anywhere; all the world would have been white from one year's end to another, all the rivers frozen tight, and all the country covered with snow and ice.

Luckily there was a limit to his power. Strong and fierce as he was, he was no match at all for Sha-won-dasee, the South Wind, whose home was in the pleasant land of the sun-flower. Where Sha-won-dasee dwelt it was always summer. When he breathed upon the land, violets appeared in the woods, the wild rose bloomed on the yellow prairie, and the cooing dove called musically to his mate. It was he who caused the melons to grow, and the purple grapes; it was he whose warm breath ripened the corn in the fields, clothed the forests in green, and made the earth all glad and beautiful. Then, as the summer days grew shorter in the North, Sha-won-dasee would climb to the top of a hill, fill his great pipe, and sit there—dreaming and smoking. Hour after hour he sat and smoked; and the smoke, rising in the form of a vapor, filled the air with a soft haze until the hills and lakes seemed like the hills and lakes of dreamland. Not a breath of wind, not a cloud in the sky; a great peace and stillness over all. Nowhere else in the world was there anything so wonderful. It was Indian Summer.

Now it was that the fishermen who set their nets in the North worked hard and fast, knowing the time was at hand when the South Wind would fall asleep, and fierce old Ka-bib-on-okka would swoop down upon them and drive them away. Sure enough! One morning a thin film of ice covered the water where they set their nets; a heavy frost sparkled in the sun on the bark roof of their huts.

That was sufficient warning. The ice grew thicker, the snow fell in big, feathery flakes. Coyote, the prairie wolf, trotted by in his shaggy white winter coat. Already they could hear a muttering and a moaning in the distance.

"Ka-bib-on-okka is coming!" cried the fishermen. "Ka-bib-on-okka will soon be here. It is time for us to go."

But Shin-ge-bis, the diver, only laughed.

Shin-ge-bis was always laughing. He laughed when he caught a big fish, and he laughed when he caught none at all. Nothing could dampen his spirits.

"The fishing is still good," he said to his comrades. "I can cut a hole in the ice, and fish with a line instead of a net. What do *I* care for old Ka-bib-on-okka?"

They looked at him with amazement. It was true that Shin-ge-bis had certain magic powers, and could change himself into a duck. They had seen him do it; and that is why he came to be called the "diver." But how would this enable him to brave the anger of the terrible North Wind?

"You had better come with us," they said. "Ka-bib-onok-ka is much stronger than you. The biggest trees of the forest bend before his wrath. The swiftest river that runs freezes at his touch. Unless you can turn yourself into a bear, or a fish, you will have no chance at all."

But Shin-ge-bis only laughed the louder.

"My fur coat lent me by Brother Beaver and my mittens borrowed from Cousin Muskrat will protect me in the day-time," he said, "and inside my wigwam is a pile of big logs. Let Ka-bib-on-okka come in by my fire if he dares."

So the fishermen took their leave rather sadly; for the laughing Shin-ge-bis was a favorite with them, and, the truth is, they never expected to see him again.

When they were gone, Shin-ge-bis set about his work in his own way. First of all he made sure that he had plenty of dry bark and twigs and pine-needles, to make the fire blaze up when he returned to his wigwam in the evening. The snow by this time was pretty deep, but it froze so hard on top that the sun did not melt it, and he could walk on the surface without sinking in at all. As for fish, he well knew how to catch them through the holes he made in the ice; and at night he would go tramping home, trailing a long string of them behind him, and singing a song he had made up himself:

> "Ka-bib-on-okka, ancient man,
> Come and scare me if you can.
> Big and blustery though you be,
> You are mortal just like me!"

It was thus that Ka-bib-on-okka found him, plodding along late one afternoon across the snow.

"Whoo, whoo!" cried the North Wind. "What impudent, two-legged creature is this who dares to linger here long after the wild goose and the heron have winged their way to the south? We shall see who is master in the Land of Ice. This very night I will force my way into his wigwam, put his fire out, and scatter the ashes all around. Whoo, whoo!"

Night came; Shin-ge-bis sat in his wigwam by the blazing fire. And such a fire! Each backlog was so big it would last for a moon. That was the way the Indians, who had no clocks or watches, counted time; instead of weeks or months, they would say "a moon"—the length of time from one new moon to another.

Shin-ge-bis had been cooking a fish, a fine, fresh fish caught that very day. Broiled over the coals, it was a tender and savory dish; and Shin-ge-bis smacked his lips, and rubbed his hands with pleasure. He had tramped many miles that day; so it was a pleasant thing to sit there by the roaring fire and toast his shins. How foolish, he thought, his comrades had been to leave a place where fish was so plentiful, so early in the winter.

"They think that Ka-bib-on-okka is a kind of magician," he was saying to himself, "and that no one can resist him. It's my own opinion that he's a man, just like myself. It's true that I can't stand the cold as he does; but then, neither can he stand the heat as I do." This thought amused him so that he began to laugh and sing:

> *"Ka-bib-on-okka, frosty man,*
> *Try to freeze me if you can.*
> *Though you blow until you tire,*
> *I am safe beside my fire!"*

He was in such a high good humor that he scarcely noticed a sudden uproar that began without. The snow came thick and fast; as it fell it was caught up again like so much powder and blown against the wigwam, where it lay in huge drifts. But instead of making it colder inside, it was really like a thick blanket that kept the air out.

Ka-bib-on-okka soon discovered his mistake, and it made him furious. Down the smoke-vent he shouted; and his voice was so wild and terrible that it might have frightened an ordinary man. But Shin-ge-bis only laughed. It was so quiet in that great, silent country that he rather enjoyed a little noise.

"Ho, ho!" he shouted back. "How are you, Ka-bib-onok-ka? If you are not careful you will burst your cheeks."

Then the wigwam shook with the force of the blast, and the curtain of buffalo hide that formed the doorway flapped and rattled, and rattled and flapped.

"Come on in, Ka-bib-on-okka!" called Shin-ge-bis merrily. "Come on in and warm yourself. It must be bitter cold outside."

At these jeering words, Ka-bib-on-okka hurled himself against the curtain, breaking one of the buckskin thongs; and made his way inside. Oh, what an icy breath! So icy that it filled the hot wigwam like a fog.

Shin-ge-bis pretended not to notice. Still singing, he rose to his feet, and threw on another log. It was a fat log of pine, and it burned so hard and gave out so much heat that he had to sit a little distance away. From the corner of his eye he watched Ka-bib-on-okka; and what he saw made him laugh again. The perspiration was pouring from his forehead; the snow and icicles in his flowing hair quickly disappeared. Just as a snowman made by children melts in the warm sun of March, so the fierce old North Wind began to thaw! There could be no doubt of it; Ka-bib-on-okka, the terrible, was melting! His nose and ears became smaller, his body began to shrink. If he remained where he was much longer, the King of the Land of Ice would be nothing better than a puddle.

"Come on up to the fire," said Shin-ge-bis cruelly. "You must be chilled to the bone. Come up closer, and warm your hands and feet."

But the North Wind had fled, even faster than he came, through the doorway.

Once outside, the cold air revived him, and all his anger returned. As he had not been able to freeze Shin-ge-bis, he spent his rage on everything in his path. Under his tread the snow took on a crust; the brittle branches of the trees snapped as he blew and snorted; the prowling fox hurried to his hole; and the wandering coyote sought the first shelter at hand.

Once more he made his way to the wigwam of Shin-ge-bis, and shouted down the flue. "Come out," he called. "Come out, if you dare, and wrestle with me here in the snow. We'll soon see who's master then!"

Shin-ge-bis thought it over. "The fire must have weakened him," he said to himself. "And my own body is warm. I believe I can overpower him. Then he will not annoy me any more, and I can stay here as long as I please."

Out of the wigwam he rushed, and Ka-bib-on-okka came to meet him. Then a great struggle took place. Over and over on the hard snow they rolled, locked in one another's arms.

All night long they wrestled; and the foxes crept out of their holes, sitting at a safe distance in a circle, watching the wrestlers. The effort he put forth kept the blood warm in the body of Shin-ge-bis. He could feel the North Wind growing weaker and weaker; his icy breath was no longer a blast, but only a feeble sigh.

At last, as the sun rose in the east, the wrestlers stood apart, panting. Ka-bib-on-okka was conquered. With a despairing wail, he turned and sped away. Far, far to the North he sped, even to the land of the White Rabbit; and as he went, the laughter of Shin-ge-bis rang out and followed him. Cheerfulness and courage can overcome even the North Wind.

THE BOY WHO
SNARED THE SUN

Deep, crusted snow covered the earth, and sparkled in the light of a wintry moon. The wind had died away; it was very cold and still. Not a sound came from the forest; the only noise that broke the perfect quiet of the night was the cracking of the ice on the Big-sea-water, Gitche Gumee, which was now frozen solid.

But inside old Iagoo's teepee it was warm and cheerful. The teepee, as the Indians call a tent, was covered with the thick, tough skin of the buffalo; the winter coat of Muk-wa, the bear, had now become a pleasant soft rug for Iagoo's two young visitors, Morning Glory and her little brother, Eagle Feather. Squatting at their ease on the warm fur, they waited for the old man to speak.

Suddenly a white-footed mouse crept from his nest in a corner, and, advancing close to the children, sat up on his hind-legs, like a dog that begs for a biscuit. Eagle Feather raised his hand in a threatening way, but Morning Glory caught him by the arm.

"No, no!" she said. "You must not harm him. See how friendly he is, and not a bit afraid. There is game enough in the forest for a brave boy's bow and arrow. Why should he spend his strength on a weak little mouse?"

Eagle Feather, pleased with anything that seemed like praise of his strength, let his hand fall. "Your words are true words, Morning Glory," he answered. "Against Ahmeek, the beaver, or Wau-be-se, the wild swan, it is better that I should measure my hunter's skill."

At this, Iagoo, turning around, broke his long silence.

"There was a time," he said, mysteriously, "when a thousand boys such as Eagle Feather would have been no match at all for that mouse as he used to be."

"When was that?" asked Eagle Feather, looking uneasily at his sister.

"In the days of the great Dormouse," answered Iagoo. "In the days, long ago, when there were many more animals than men on the earth, and the biggest of all the beasts was the Dormouse. Then something strange happened—something that never happened before or since. Shall I tell you about it?"

"O, please do!" begged Morning Glory.

"The story I am going to tell you," began Iagoo, "is not so much a story about the Dormouse as it is a story about a little boy and his sister. Yet had it not been for the Dormouse, I would not be here to tell about it, and you would not be here to listen.

"To begin with, you must understand that the world in those days was a different sort of place from what it is now.

O yes, a different sort of place. People did not eat the flesh of animals. They lived on berries, and roots, and wild vegetables. The Great Spirit, who made all things on land, and in the sky and water, had not yet given men Mon-da-min, the Indian corn. There was no fire to give them heat, or to cook with. In all the world there was just one small fire, watched by two old witches who let nobody come near it; and until Coyote, the prairie wolf, came along and stole some of this fire, the food that people could manage to get was eaten raw, the way it grew."

"They must have been pretty hungry," said Morning Glory.

"O, yes, they were hungry," agreed Iagoo. "But that was

not all. There were so many animals, and so few men, that the animals ruled the earth in their own way. The biggest of them all was Bosh-kwa-dosh, the Mastodon. He was higher than the highest trees, and he had an enormous appetite. But he did not stay long on earth, or there would not have been food enough even for the other animals."

"I thought you said the Dormouse was the biggest," interrupted Eagle Feather.

Iagoo looked at him severely.

"At the time I speak of," he continued, "Bosh-kwa-dosh, the Mastodon, had just gone away. He had not gone a bit too soon, either; for, by this time, the only people left on the whole earth were a young girl and her little brother."

"Like Eagle Feather and me?" asked Morning Glory. "The girl was much like you," said Iagoo, patiently. "But the boy was a dwarf, who never grew to be more than three feet high. Being so much stronger and larger than her brother, she gathered all the food for both, and cared for him in every way. Sometimes she would take him along with her, when she went to look for berries and roots. 'He's such a very little boy,' she said to herself, 'that if I leave him all alone, some big bird may swoop down, and carry him off to its nest.'

"She did not know what a strange boy he was, and how much mischief he could do when he set his mind upon it. One day she said to him: 'Look, little brother! I have made you a bow and some arrows. It is time you learned to take care of yourself; so when I am gone, practice shooting, for this is a thing you must know how to do.'

"Winter was coming, and to keep himself from freezing the boy had nothing better than a light garment woven by his sister from the wild grasses. How could he get a warm coat?

As he asked himself that question, a flock of snow birds flew down, near by, and began pecking at the fallen logs, to get the worms. 'Ha!' said he. 'Their feathers would make me a fine coat.' Bending his bow, he let an arrow fly; but he had not yet learned how to shoot straight. It went wide of the mark. He shot a second, and a third; then the birds took fright, and flew away.

"Each day he tried again—shooting at a tree when there was nothing better to aim at. At last he killed a snow bird, then another and another. When he had shot ten birds, he had enough. 'See, sister,' he said, 'I shall not freeze. Now you can make me a coat from the skins of these little birds.'

"So his sister sewed the skins together, and made him the coat, the first warm winter coat he had ever had. It was fine to look at, and the feathers kept out the cold. Eh-yah! he was proud of it! With his bow and arrows, he strutted up and down, like a little turkey cock. 'Is it true?' he asked, 'that you and I are the only persons living on earth? Perhaps if I look around, I may find someone else. It will do no harm to try.'

"His sister feared he would come to some harm; but he had made up his mind to see the world for himself, and off he went. But his legs were short, he was not used to walking far, and he soon grew tired. When he came to a bare place, on the edge of a hill, where the sun had melted the snow, he lay down, and was soon fast asleep.

"As he slept, the sun played him a trick. It was a mild winter's day. The bird skins of which the coat was made were still fresh and tender, and under the full glare of the sun they began to shrivel and shrink. 'Eh-yah! What's wrong?' he muttered in his sleep, feeling the coat become tighter and tighter. Then he woke, stretched out his arms, and saw what had happened.

"The sun was nearly sinking now. The boy stood up and faced it, and shook his small fist. 'See what you have done!' he cried, with a stamp of his foot. 'You have spoiled my new birdskin coat. Never mind! You think yourself beyond my reach, up there; but I'll be revenged on you. Just wait and see!'"

"But how could he reach the sun?" asked Morning Glory, her eyes growing rounder and rounder.

"That is what his sister asked, when he told her about it," said Iagoo. "And what do you think he did? First, he did nothing at all but stretch himself out on the ground, where he lay for ten days without eating or moving. Then he turned over on the other side, and lay there for ten days more. At last he rose to his feet. 'I have made up my mind,' he said. 'Sister, I have a plan to catch the sun in a noose. Find me some kind of a cord from which I can make a snare.' "She got some tough grass, and twisted it into a rope. 'That will not do,' he said. 'You must find something stronger.' He no longer talked like a little boy, but like one who was to be obeyed. Then his sister thought of her hair. She cut enough from her head to make a cord, and when she had plaited it he was much pleased, and said it would do. He took it from her, and drew it between his lips, and as he did this it turned into a kind of metal, and grew much stronger and longer, till he had so much that he wound it around his body.

"In the middle of the night he made his way to the hill, and there he fixed a noose at the place where the sun would rise. He had to wait a long time in the cold and darkness. But at last a faint light came into the sky. As the sun rose it was caught fast in the noose, and there it stayed."

Iagoo stopped talking, and sat looking into the fire. One might have supposed that when he did this he saw pictures in the flames, and in the red coals, and that these pictures helped him to tell the story. But Morning Glory was impatient to hear the rest.

"Iagoo," she said, timidly, at last. "Did you forget about the Dormouse?"

"Eh-yah! the Dormouse! No. I have not forgotten," answered the old man, rousing himself. "When the sun did not rise as usual, the animals could not tell what had happened. Ad-ji-dau-mo, the squirrel, chattered and scolded from the branch of a pine tree. Kah-gah-gee, the raven, flapped his wings, and croaked more hoarsely than ever, to tell the others that the end of the world had come. Only Muk-wa, the bear, did not mind. He had crept into his cave for the winter, and the darker it was the better he liked it.

"Wa-bun, the East Wind, was the one who brought the news. He had drawn from his quiver the silver arrows with which he chased the darkness from the valleys. But the sun had not risen to help him, and the arrows fell harmless to the earth. 'Wake, wake!' he wailed. 'Someone has caught the sun in a snare. Which of all the animals will dare to cut the cord?'

"But even Coyote, the prairie wolf, who was the wisest of them all, could think of no way to free the sun. So great was the heat thrown out by its rays that he could not come within an arrow's flight of where it was caught fast in the magical noose of hair.

"'Leave it to me!' screamed Ken-eu, the war-eagle, from his nest on the cliff. 'It is I alone who soar to the sky, and look the sun in the face, without winking. Leave it to me!'

"Down he darted through the darkness, and up he flew

again, with his eagle feathers singed. Then they woke the Dormouse. They had a hard time doing it, because when he once went to sleep he stayed asleep for six months, and it was almost impossible to arouse him. Coyote crept close to his ear, and howled with all his might. It would have split the eardrum of almost any other animal. But Kug-e-been-gwa-kwa, the Dormouse, only groaned and turned over on the other side, and Coyote had a narrow escape from being mashed flat, like a corn-cake.

"'There is only one thing that will wake him,' said Coyote, getting up and shaking himself. 'I will run to the mountain cave of An-ne-mee-kee, the Thunder. His voice is even more terrible than mine.' So off he went at a gallop.

"Soon they could hear An-ne-mee-kee coming. Boom, boom! When he shouted in the ear of the Dormouse, the biggest beast on earth rose slowly to his feet. In the darkness he looked bigger than ever, almost as big as a mountain. An-ne-mee-kee, the Thunder, shouted once more, to make sure that the Dormouse was really wide awake, and would not go to sleep again.

"'Now,' said Coyote to the Dormouse, 'it is you that will have to free the sun. If he burned one of us, there would be little left but bones. But you are so big that if part of you is burned away there will still be enough. Then, in that case you would not have to eat so much, or work so hard to get it.'

"The Dormouse was a stupid animal, and Coyote's talk seemed true talk. Besides, as he was the biggest animal, he was expected to do the biggest things. So he made his way to the hill, where the little boy had snared the sun, and began to nibble at the noose. As he nibbled away, his back got hotter and hotter. Soon it began to burn, till all the upper part of him burned away, and became great heaps of ashes. At last, when he had cut through the cord with his teeth, and set the sun free, all that was left of him was an animal no larger than an ordinary mouse. What he became then, so he is today. Still, he is big enough for a mouse; and perhaps that is what Coyote really meant. Coyote, the prairie wolf, is a cunning beast, up to many tricks, and it is not always easy to tell exactly what he means."

HOW THE SUMMER CAME

Morning Glory was tired of the winter, and longed for the spring to come. Sometimes it seemed as if Ka-bib-on-okka, the fierce old North Wind, would never go back to his home in the Land of Ice. With his cold breath he had frozen tight and hard the Big-Sea-Water,Gitche Gumee, and covered it deep with snow, till you could not tell the Great Lake from the land.

Except for the beautiful green pines, all the world was white—a dazzling, silent world in which there was no musical murmur of waters and no song of birds.

"Will O-pee-chee, the robin, never come again?" sighed Morning Glory. "Suppose there was no summer anywhere, and no Sha-won-dasee, the South Wind, to bring the violet and the dove. O, Iagoo, would it not be dreadful?"

"Be patient, Morning Glory," answered the old man. "Soon you will hear Wa-wa, the wild goose, flying high up, on his way to the North. I have lived many moons. Sometimes he seems long in coming, but he always comes. When you hear him call, then O-pee-chee, the robin, will not be far behind."

"I'll try to be patient" said Morning Glory. "But Ka-bib-on-okka, the North wnd, is so strong and fierce. I can't help wondering whether there ever was a time when his power was so great that he made his home here always. It makes me shiver to think of it!"

Iagoo rose from his place by the fire, and drew to one side the curtain of buffalo-hide that screened the doorway. He pointed to the sky—clear, and sparkling with stars.

"Look!" he said. "There, in the North. See that little cluster of stars. Do you know the name we give it?"

"I know," said Eagle Feather. "It is O-jeeg An-nung—the Fisher stars. If you look right, you can see how they make the body of the Fisher. He is stretched out flat, with an arrow through his tail. See, sister!"

"The Fisher," repeated Morning Glory. "You mean the furry little animal, something like a fox? Is Marten another name for it?"

"That's it," said Eagle Feather.

"Yes, I see," nodded Morning Glory. "But why is the Fisher spread out flat that way, in the sky, with an arrow sticking through his tail?"

"I don't know just exactly why," admitted Eagle Feather. "I suppose some hunter was chasing him. Perhaps Iagoo can tell us."

Iagoo closed the curtain, and went back to the fire.

"You thought there might have been a time when there was no summer on the earth," he said to Morning Glory. "And you were right. Until O-jeeg, the Fisher, found a way to bring the summer down from the sky, the earth was everywhere covered with snow, and it was always cold. If O-jeeg had not been willing to give his life, so that all the rest of us could be warm, Ka-bib-on-okka, the North Wind, would have ruled the world, as he now rules the Land of Ice."

Then Morning Glory and Eagle Feather sat down on the soft rug that was once the winter coat of Muk-wa, the bear, and Iagoo told them the story of How the Summer Came:

In the wild forest that borders the Great Lake there once lived a mighty hunter named O-jeeg. No one knew the woods so well as he; where others would be lost without a trail to guide them, he found his way easily and quickly, by day or night, through the trackless tangle of trees and underbrush. Where the red deer fled, he followed; the bear could not escape his swift pursuit. He had the cunning of the fox, the endurance of the wolf, the speed of the wild turkey when it runs at the scent of danger.

When O-jeeg shot an arrow, it always hit the mark. When he set out on a journey, no storm or snow could turn him back. He did everything he said he would do, and did it well. Thus it was that some men came to believe that O-jeeg was a Manito—the Indian name for one who has magic powers. This much was certain: whenever O-jeeg wished to do so, he could change himself into the little animal known as the Fisher, or Marten.

Perhaps that is why he was on such friendly terms with some of the animals, who were always willing to help him when he called upon them. Among these were the otter, the beaver, the lynx, the badger and the wolverine. There came a time, as we shall see, when he needed their services badly, and they were not slow in coming to his assistance.

O-jeeg had a wife whom he dearly loved, and a son, of thirteen years, who promised to be as great a hunter as his father. Already he had shown great skill with the bow and arrow; if some accident should prevent O-jeeg from supplying the family with the game upon which they lived, his son felt sure that he himself could shoot as many squirrels and turkeys as they needed to keep them from starving. With O-jeeg to bring them venison, bear's meat and wild turkey, they had thus far plenty to eat. Had it not been for the cold, the boy would have been happy enough. They had warm clothing, made from deerskin and furs; to keep their fire burning, they had all the wood in the forest. Yet, in spite of this, the cold was a great trial; for it was always winter, and the deep snow never melted.

Some wise old men had somewhere heard that the sky was not only the roof of our own world, but also was the floor of a beautiful world beyond; a land where birds with bright feathers sang sweetly through a pleasant, warm season called Summer. It was a pretty story that people wished to believe; and likely enough they said, when you came to think that the sun was so far away from the earth, and so close to the sky itself.

The boy used to dream about it, and wonder what could be done. His father could do anything; some men said he was a Manito. Perhaps he could find some way to bring Summer to the earth. That would be the greatest thing of all.

Sometimes it was so cold that when the boy went into the woods his fingers would be frost-bitten. Then he could not fit the notch of his arrow to the bowstring, and was obliged to go back home without any game whatever. One day he had wandered far in the forest, and was returning emptyhanded, when he saw a red squirrel seated on his hind-legs on the stump of a tree. The squirrel was gnawing a pine cone, and did not try to run away when the young hunter came near. Then the little animal spoke:

"My grandson," said he, "there is something I wish to tell you that you will be pleased to hear. Put away your arrows, and do not try to shoot me, and I shall give you some good advice."

The boy was surprised; but he unstrung his bow, and put the arrow in his quiver.

"Now," said the squirrel, "listen carefully to what I have to say. The earth is always covered with snow, and the frost bites your fingers, and makes you unhappy. I dislike the cold as much as you do. To tell the truth, there is little enough for me to eat in these woods, with the ground frozen hard all the time. You can see how thin I am, for there is not much to eat in a pine cone. If someone could manage to bring the Summer down from the sky, it would be a great blessing." "Is it really true, then," asked the boy, "that up beyond the sky is a pleasant warm land, where Winter only stays for a few moons?"

"Yes, it is true," said the squirrel. "We animals have known it for a long time. Ken-eu, the war-eagle, who soars near the sun, once saw a small crack in the sky. The crack was made by Way-wass-i-mo, the Lightning, in a great storm that covered all the earth with water. Ken-eu, the war-eagle, felt the warm air leaking through; but the people who live up above mended the crack the very next moment, and the sky has never leaked again."

"Then our wise old men were right," said the boy. "O-jeeg, my father, can do most anything he has a mind to. Do you suppose if he tried hard enough, he could get through the sky, and bring the Summer down to us?"

"Of course!" exclaimed the squirrel. "That is why I spoke to you about it. Your father is a Manito. If you beg him hard enough, and tell him how unhappy you are, he is sure to make the attempt. When you go back, show him your frostbitten fingers. Tell him how you tramp all day through the snow, and how difficult it is to make your way home. Tell him that some day you may be frozen stiff, and never get back at all. Then he will do as you ask, because he loves you very much."

The boy thanked the squirrel, and promised to follow this advice. From that day he gave his father no peace. At last O-jeeg said to him:

"My son, what you ask me to do is a dangerous thing, and I do not know what may come of it. But my power as a Manito was given me for a good purpose, and I can put it to no better use than to try to bring the Summer down from the sky, and make the world a more pleasant place to live in." Then he prepared a feast to which he invited his friends, the otter, the beaver, the lynx, the badger, and the wolverine; and they all put their heads together, to decide what was best to be done. The lynx was the first to speak. He had travelled far on his long legs, and had been to many strange places.

Besides, if you had good strong eyes, and you looked at the sky, on a clear night when there was no moon, you could see a little group of stars which the wise old men said was exactly like a lynx. It gave him a certain importance, especially in matters of this kind; so when he began to speak, the others listened with great respect.

"There is a high mountain," said he, "that none of you has ever seen. No one ever saw the top, because it is always hidden by the clouds; but I am told it is the highest mountain in the world, and almost touches the sky."

The otter began to laugh. He is the only animal that can do this; sometimes he laughs for no particular reason, unless it is that he thinks himself more clever than the other animals, and likes to "show off."

"What are you laughing at?" asked the lynx.

"Oh, nothing," answered the otter. "I was just laughing."

"It will get you into trouble some day," said the lynx. "Just because you never heard of this mountain, you think it is not there."

"Do you know how to get to it?" asked O-jeeg. "If we could climb to the top, we might find a way to break through the sky. It seems a good plan."

"That is what I was thinking," said the lynx. "It is true I don't know just where it is. But a moon's journey from here, there lives a Manito who has the shape of a giant. *He* knows, and he could tell us."

So O-jeeg bade good-bye to his wife and his little son, and the next day the lynx began the long journey, with O-jeeg and the others following close behind. It was just as the lynx had said. When they had travelled, day and night, for a moon, they came to a lodge, as the white men call an Indian's tent; and there was the Manito standing in the doorway. He was a queer-looking man, such as they had never seen before, with an enormous head and three eyes, one eye being set in his forehead above the other two.

He invited them into the lodge, and set some meat before them; but he had such an odd look, and his movements were so awkward, that the otter could not help laughing. At this, the eye in the Manito's forehead grew red, like a live coal, and he made a leap at the otter, who barely managed to slip through the doorway, out into the bitter cold and darkness of the night, without having tasted a morsel of supper. When the otter had gone, the Manito seemed satisfied, and told them they could spend the night in his lodge. They did so; and O-jeeg, who stayed awake while his friends slept, noticed that only two of the Manito's eyes were closed, while the one in his forehead remained wide open.

In the morning the Manito told O-jeeg to travel straight toward the North Star, and that in twenty suns—the Indian name for days—they would reach the mountain. "As you are a Manito yourself," he said, "you may be able to climb to the top, and to take your friends with you. But I cannot promise that you will be able to get down again."

"If it is close enough to the sky," answered O-jeeg, "that is all I ask."

Once more they set out. On their way they met the otter, who laughed again when he saw them; but this time he laughed because he was glad to find them, and glad to get some meat that O-jeeg had saved from the Manito's supper.

In twenty days they came to the foot of the mountain. Then up and up they climbed, till they passed quite through the clouds; up once more, till at last they stopped, all out of breath, and sat down to rest on the highest peak in the world. To their great delight, the sky seemed so close that they could almost touch it.

O-jeeg and his comrades filled their pipes. But before smoking, they called out to the Great Spirit, asking for success in their attempt. In Indian fashion they pointed to the earth, to the sky overhead, and to the four winds.

"Now," said O-jeeg, when they had finished smoking, "which of you can jump the highest?"

The otter grinned.

"Jump, then!" commanded O-jeeg.

The otter jumped, and, sure enough, his head hit the sky. But the sky was the harder of the two, and back he fell When he struck the ground, he began to slide down the mountain; soon he was out of sight, and they saw him no more.

"Ugh!" grunted the lynx. "He is laughing on the other side of his mouth."

It was the beaver's turn. He, too, hit the sky, but fell down in a heap. The badger and the lynx had no better luck, and their heads ached for a long time afterward.

"It all depends on you," said O-jeeg to the wolverine. "You are the strongest of them all. Ready, now—jump!" The wolverine jumped, and fell, but came down on his feet, sound and whole.

"Good!" cried O-jeeg. "Try again!"

This time the wolverine made a dent in the sky.

"It's cracking!" exclaimed O-jeeg. "Now, once more!" For the third time the wolverine jumped. Through the sky he went, passing out of sight, and O-jeeg quickly followed him.

Looking around them, they beheld a beautiful land.

O-jeeg, who had spent his life among the snows, stood like a man who dreams, wondering if it could be true. He had left behind him a bare world, white with winter, whose waters were always frozen, a world without song or color. He had now come into a country that was a great green plain, with flowers of many hues; where birds of bright plumage sang amid the leafy branches of trees hung with golden fruit. Streams wandered through the meadows, and flowed into lovely lakes. The air was mild, and filled with the perfume from a million blossoms. It was Summer.

Along the banks of a lake were the lodges in which lived the people of the sky, who could be seen some distance away. The lodges were empty, but before them were hung cages in which there were many beautiful birds. Already the warm air of Summer had begun to rush through the hole made by the wolverine, and O-jeeg now made haste to open the cages, so that the birds could follow.

The sky-dwellers saw what was happening, and raised a great shout. But Spring, Summer and Autumn had already escaped through the opening into the world below, and many of the birds as well.

The wolverine, too, had managed to reach the hole, and descend to the earth, before the sky-dwellers could catch him. But O-jeeg was not so fortunate. There were still some birds remaining that he knew his son would like to see, so he went on opening the cages. By this time the sky dwellers had closed the hole, and O-jeeg was too late.

As the sky-dwellers pursued him, he changed himself into the Fisher, and ran along the plain, toward the North, at the top of his speed. In the form of the Fisher he could run faster. Also, when he took this shape, no arrow could injure him unless it hit a spot near the tip of his tail.

But the sky-dwellers ran even faster, and the Fisher climbed a tall tree. They were good marksmen, and they shot a great many arrows, until at last one of these chanced to hit the fatal spot. Then the Fisher knew that his time had come.

Now he saw that some of his enemies were marked with the totems, or family arms, of his own tribe. "My Cousins!" he called to them. "I beg of you that you go away, and leave me here alone."

The sky-dwellers granted his request. When they had gone, the Fisher came down from the tree, and wandered around for a time, seeking some opening in the plain through which he might return to the earth. But there was no opening; so at last, feeling weak and faint, he stretched himself flat on the floor of the sky, through which the stars may be seen from the world below.

"I have kept my promise," he said with a sigh of content. "My son will now enjoy the summer, and so will all the people who dwell on the earth. Through the ages to come I shall be set as a sign in the heavens, and my name will be spoken with praise. I am satisfied."

So it came about that the Fisher remained in the sky, where you can see him plainly for yourself, on a clear night, with the arrow through his tail. The Indians call them the Fisher Stars—O-jeeg An-nung; but to white men are they known as the constellation of the Plough.

THE FAIRY BRIDE

Once there was a lovely young girl named Neen-i-zu, the only daughter of an Indian chief, who lived on the shore of Lake Superior; Neen-i-zu, in the Indian language, means "My Dear Life." It was plain that her parents loved her tenderly, and did everything in their power to make her happy and to shield her from any possible harm.

There was but one thing that made them uneasy. Neen-i-zu was a favorite with the other young girls of the village, and joined them in their play. But she liked best of all to walk by herself in the forest, or to follow some dim trail that led to the heart of the little hills. Sometimes she would be absent for many hours; and when she returned, her eyes had the look of one who has dwelt in secret places, and seen things strange and mysterious. Nowadays, some persons would have called Neen-i-zu "romantic." Others, who can never see a thing that is not just beneath their noses, would have laughed a little, in a superior sort of way, and said she was a "dreamer." What was it that Neen-i-zu saw and heard, during these lonely walks in the secret places of the hills? Was it perhaps the fairies? She did not say. But her mother, who wished her to be more like other girls, and who would have liked to see her marry and settle down, was much disturbed in mind.

The mischievous little fairies known as Puk-Wudjies were believed to inhabit the sand dunes where Neen-i-zu so often went to walk. These were the sand-hills made by Grasshopper, when he danced so madly at Man-a-bo-zho's wedding, whirling the sand into great drifts and mounds that may be seen to this very day. The Puk-Wudjies loved these hills, which were seldom visited by the Indians. It was just the place for leap-frog and all-hands-'round; in the twilight of summer days they were said to gather here in little bands, playing all manner of pranks. Then, as night came, they would make haste to hide themselves in a grove of pine-trees known as the *Manito Wac*, or the Wood of the Spirits.

No one had ever come close to them; but fishermen, paddling their canoes on the lake, had caught glimpses of them from afar, and had heard the tiny voices of these merry little men, as they laughed and called to one another. When the fishermen tried to follow, the Puk-Wudjies would vanish in the woods; but their foot-prints, no larger than a child's, could be seen on the damp sand of a little lake in the hills.

If anything more were needed to convince those doubters who did not believe in fairies, the proof was quickly supplied by fishermen and hunters who were victims of their tricks. The Puk-Wudjies never really harmed anyone, but they were up to many kinds of mischief. Sometimes a hunter, picking up his cap in the morning, would find the feathers plucked out; sometimes a fisherman, missing his paddle, would discover it at last in a tree. When such things happened it was perfectly plain that Puk-Wudjies had been up to their pranks, and few persons were still stupid enough to believe it could be anything else.

Neen-i-zu had her own ideas concerning these little men; for she, like Morning Glory, had often listened to the tales that old Iagoo told. One of these stories was the story of a Happy Land, a far-off place where it was always Summer; where no one wept or suffered sorrow.

It was for this land that she sighed. It filled her thoughts by day, when she sought the secret places of the hills, and sat in some lonely spot, listening to the mysterious voices that whispered in the breeze. Where was this Happy Land—this place without pain or care?

Tired out at night, she would sink into her bed. Then from their hiding places would come stealing the small messengers of Weenz, the Spirit of Sleep. These kindly gnomes— too small for the human eye to see—crept quickly up the face of the weary Neen-i-zu and tapped gently on her forehead with their tiny war-clubs, called *pub-ga-mau-guns*. Taptap— tap!—till her eyelids closed, and she sought the Happy Land in that other pleasant land of dreams.

She, too, had seen the foot-prints of the Puk-Wudjies on the sandy beach of the little lake, and had heard their merry laughter ring out in the grove of pines. Was it their only dwelling place, she asked herself, or were they not messengers from the Happy Land, sent to show the way to that mortal who believed in it, and longed to enter.

Neen-i-zu came to think that this must be really so. Oftener than ever, she made her way to the meadow bordering on the Spirit Wood, and sat there gazing into the grove. Perhaps the Puk-Wudjies would understand, and tell the fairies whom they served. Then some day a fairy would appear at the edge of the pines, and beckon her to come. That would surely happen, she thought, if she wished it long enough, and could give her wishes wings. So, sitting there, she composed the words of a song, and set it to the music the pines make when the south wind stirs their branches. Then she sang:

Spirit of the laughing leaves,
Fairy of the forest pine,
Listen to the maid who grieves
For that happy land of thine.

From your haunt in summer glade
Hasten to your mournful maid.

Was it only her fancy, that she seemed to hear the clos-
ing words of her song echoed from the deep woods where the
merry little men had vanished? Or was it the Puk-Wudjies
mocking her?

She had lingered later than usual; it was time to go. The
new moon swung low in the western sky, with its points turned
upwards to the heavens. An Indian would say he could hang
his powder horn upon it, and that it meant dry weather, when
the leaves crackled under the hunter's feet, and the animals
fled before him, so that he was unable to come near-enough
to shoot. And Neen-i-zu was glad of this. In the Happy Land,
she declared no one would suffer, and no life would be taken.

Yet it was a hunter that her mother wished her to marry,
a man who spent his whole life in slaying the red deer of the
forest; who thought and talked of almost nothing else.

This came into her mind as she rose from her seat in the
meadow, and cast a farewell glance at the pines. The rays of
the crescent moon touched them with a faint light; and again
her fancy came into play. What was it that seemed to move
along the edge of the mysterious woods? Something with the
dim likeness of a youth—taller than the Puk-Wudjies—who
glided rather than walked, and whose garments of light green
stood out against the darker green of the pines. Neeni-zu
looked again; but the moon hid behind the hills. All was black
to the eye; to the ear came no sound but the creepy cry of the
whip-poor-will. She hastened home.

That night she heard from her mother's lips what she
had long expected and feared. "Neen-i-zu," said her mother.

"I named you 'My dear Life,' and you are as dear as life to me. That is why I wish you to be safe and happy. That is why I wish you to marry a good man who will take the best care of you now, and will protect and comfort you when I am gone. You know the man I mean."

"Yes, mother," answered Neen-i-zu. "I know him well enough—as well as ever I want to know him. He hunts the deer, he kills the deer, he skins the deer. That is all he does, that is all he thinks, that is all he talks about. It is perhaps well that someone should do this, lest we starve for want of meat. Yet there are many other things in the world, and this hunter of yours is content if he does but kill."

"Poor child!" said her mother. "You are too young to know what is best for you."

"I am old enough, mother dear," answered Neen-i-zu, "to know what my heart tells me. Besides, this hunter you would have me marry is as tall as a young oak, while I am not much taller than one of the Puk-Wudjies. When I stand up very straight, my head comes little higher than his waist. A pretty pair we would make!"

What she said was quite true. Neen-i-zu had never grown to be much larger than a child. She had a graceful, slender body, little hands and feet, eyes black as midnight, and a mouth like a meadow flower. One who saw her for the first time, passing upon the hills, her slight figure sketched against the sky, might have thought that she herself was a fairy.

For all her gentle, quiet ways, and her love of lonely places, Neen-i-zu was often merry. But now she seldom laughed; her step was slow; and she walked with her eyes fixed upon the ground. "When she is married," thought her mother, "she will have other things to occupy her mind, and she will no longer go dreaming among the hills."

But the hills were her one great joy—the hills, and the flowery meadows where the lark swayed to and fro, bidding her be of good cheer, as he perched on a mullein stalk. Every afternoon she sat, singing her little song. Soon she would sing no more. The setting sun would gild the pine grove, the whip-poor-will would complain to the stars; but the picture would be incomplete; there would be no Neen-i-zu. For the wedding day was named; she must be the hunter's wife.

On this day set for her marriage to the man she so disliked, Neen-i-zu put on the garments of a bride. Never had she looked so lovely. Blood-red blossoms flamed in her jet-black hair; in her hand she held a bunch of meadow flowers mingled with the tassels of the pine.

Thus arrayed, she set out for a farewell visit to the grove. It was a thing they could not well deny her; but as she went her way, and the hills hid her from sight, the wedding guests looked uneasily at one another. It was something they could not explain. At that moment a cloud blew up from nowhere, across the sun; where light had been there was now a shadow. Was it a sign? They glanced sidelong at the hunter, but the bridegroom was sharpening his sheath knife on a stone. Sunshine or shadow, his thoughts were following the deer.

Time passed; but Neen-i-zu did not return. Then so late was the hour, that the wedding guests wondered and bestirred themselves. What could be keeping her so long? At last they searched the hills; she was not there. They tracked her to the meadow, where the prints of her little moccasins led on and on—into the grove itself; then the tracks disappeared. Neen-i-zu had vanished.

They never saw her more. The next day a hunter brought

them strange news. He had climbed a hill, on his way home by a short cut, and had paused there a moment to look around. Just then his dog ran up to him, whining, with its tail between its legs. It was a brave dog, he said, that would not run from a bear, but this one acted as if he had seen something that was not mortal.

Then the hunter heard a voice, singing. Soon the singing stopped, and he made out—far off—the figure of Neen-i-zu, walking straight toward the grove, with her arms held out before her. He called to her, but she did not hear, and drew nearer and nearer to the Spirit wood.

"She walked like one who dreams," said the hunter, "and when she had almost reached the woods, a young man, slender as a reed, came out to meet her. He was not one of our tribe. No, no! I have never seen his like. He was dressed in the leaves of the forest, and green plumes nodded on his head. He took her by the hand. They entered the Sacred Grove. There is no doubt that he was a fairy—the fairy Evergreen. There is nothing more; I have finished."

So Neen-i-zu became a bride, after all.

KANA'TI AND SELU: THE ORIGIN OF GAME AND CORN

When I was a boy this is what the old men told me they had heard when they were boys.

Long years ago, soon after the world was made, a hunter and his wife lived at Pilot knob with their only child, a little boy. The father's name was Kana'ti (The Lucky Hunter), and his wife was called Selu (Corn). No matter when Kana'ti went into the wood, he never failed to bring back a load of game, which his wife would cut up and prepare, washing off the blood from the meat in the river near the house. The little boy used to play down by the river every day, and one morning the old people thought they heard laughing and talking in the bushes as though there were two children there. When the boy came home at night his parents asked him who had been playing with him all day. "He comes out of the water," said the boy, "and he calls himself my elder brother. He says his mother was cruel to him and threw him into the river." Then they knew that the strange boy had sprung from the blood of the game which Selu had washed off at the river's edge.

Every day when the little boy went out to play the other would join him, but as he always went back again into the water the old people never had a chance to see him. At last one evening Kana'ti said to his son, "Tomorrow, when the other boy comes to play, get him to wrestle with you, and when you have your arms around him hold on to him and call for us." The boy promised to do as he was told, so the next day as soon as his playmate appeared he challenged him to a wrestling match. The other agreed at once, but as soon as they had their arms around each other, Kana'ti's boy began to scream for his father. The old folks at once came running down, and as soon as the Wild Boy saw them he struggled to free himself and cried out, "Let me go; you threw me away!" but his brother held on until the parents reached the spot, when they seized the Wild Boy and took him home with them. They kept him in the house until they had tamed him, but he was always wild and artful in his disposition, and was the leader of his brother in every mischief. It was not long until the old people discovered that he had magic powers, and they called him I'nage-utasûñ'hi (He-who-grew-up-wild).

Whenever Kana'ti went into the mountains he always brought back a fat buck or doe, or maybe a couple of turkeys. One day the Wild Boy said to his brother, "I wonder where our father gets all that game; let's follow him next time and find out." A few days afterward Kana'ti took a bow and some feathers in his hand and started off toward the west. The boys waited a little while and then went after him, keeping out of sight until they saw him go into a swamp where there were a great many of the small reeds that hunters use to make arrow-shafts. Then the Wild Boy changed himself into a puff of bird's down, which the wind took up and carried until it alighted upon Kana'ti's shoulder just as he entered the swamp, but Kana'ti knew nothing about it. The old man cut reeds, fitted the feathers to them and made some arrows, and the Wild Boy— in his other shape—thought, "I wonder what those things are for?" When Kana'ti had his arrows finished he came out of the swamp and went on again. The wind blew the down from his shoulder, and it fell in the woods, when the Wild Boy took his right shape again and went back and told his brother what he had seen. Keeping out of sight of their father, they followed him up the mountain until he stopped at a certain place and lifted a large rock. At once there ran out a buck, which Kana'ti shot, and then lifting it upon his back he started for home again. "Oho!" exclaimed the boys, "he keeps all the deer shut up in that hole, and whenever he wants meat he just lets one out and kills it with those things he made in the swamp." They hurried and reached home before their father, who had the heavy deer to carry, and he never knew that they had followed.

A few days later the boys went back to the swamp, cut some reeds, and made seven arrows, and then started up the mountain to where their father kept the game. When they got to the place, they raised the rock and a deer came running out. Just as they drew back to shoot it, another came out, and then another and another, until the boys got confused and forgot what they were about. In those days all the deer had their tails hanging down like other animals, but as a buck was running past the Wild Boy struck its tail with his arrow so that it pointed upward. The boys thought this good sport, and when the next one ran past the Wild Boy struck its tail so that it stood straight up, and his brother struck the next one so hard with his arrow that the deer's tail was almost curled over his back. The deer carries his tail this way ever since. The deer came running past until the last one had come out of the hole and escaped into the forest. Then came droves of raccoons, rabbits, and all the other four-footed animals—all but the bear, because there was no bear then. Last came great flocks of turkeys, pigeons, and partridges that darkened the air like a cloud and made such a noise with their wings that Kana'ti, sitting at home, heard the sound like distant thunder on the mountains and said to himself, "My bad boys have got into trouble; I must go and see what they are doing."

So he went up the mountain, and when he came to the

place where he kept the game he found the two boys standing by the rock, and all the birds and animals were gone. Kana'ti was furious, but without saying a word he went down into the cave and kicked the covers off four jars in one corner, when out swarmed bedbugs, fleas, lice, and gnats, and got all over the boys. They screamed with pain and fright and tried to beat off the insects, but the thousands of vermin crawled over them and bit and stung them until both dropped down nearly dead. Kana'ti stood looking on until he thought they had been punished enough, when he knocked off the vermin and made the boys a talk. "Now, you rascals," said he, "you have always had plenty to eat and never had to work for it. Whenever you were hungry all I had to do was to come up here and get a deer or a turkey and bring it home for your mother to cook; but now you have let out all the animals, and after this when you want a deer to eat you will have to hunt all over the woods for it, and then maybe not find one. Go home now to your mother, while I see if I can find something to eat for supper."

When the boys got home again they were very tired and hungry and asked their mother for something to eat. "There is no meat," said Selu, "but wait a little while and I'll get you something." So she took a basket and started out to the storehouse. This storehouse was built upon poles high up from the ground, to keep it out of the reach of animals, and there was a ladder to climb up by, and one door, but no other opening. Every day when Selu got ready to cook the dinner she would go out to the storehouse with a basket and bring it back full of corn and beans. The boys had never been inside the storehouse, so wondered where all the corn and beans could come from, as the house was not a very large one; so as soon as Selu went out of the door the Wild Boy said to his brother, "Let's go and see what she does." They ran around and climbed up at the back of the storehouse and pulled out a piece of clay from between the logs, so that they could look in. There they saw Selu standing in the middle of the room with the basket in front of her on the floor. Leaning over the basket, she rubbed her stomach—so—and the basket was half full of corn. Then she rubbed under her armpits—so—and the basket was full to the top with beans. The boys looked at each other and said, "This will never do; our mother is a witch. If we eat any of that it will poison us. We must kill her."

When the boys came back into the house, she knew their thoughts before they spoke. "So you are going to kill me?" said Selu. "Yes," said the boys, "you are a witch." "Well," said their mother, "when you have killed me, clear a large piece of ground in front of the house and drag my body seven times around the circle. Then drag me seven times over the ground inside the circle, and stay up all night and watch, and in the morning you will have plenty of corn." The boys killed her with their clubs, and cut off her head and put it up on the roof of the house with her face turned to the west, and told her to look for her husband. Then they set to work to clear the ground in front of the house, but instead of clearing the whole piece they cleared only seven little spots. This is why corn now grows only in a few places instead of over the whole world. They dragged the body of Selu around the circle, and wherever her blood fell on the ground the corn sprang up. But instead of dragging her body seven times across the ground they dragged it over only twice, which is the reason the Indians still work their crop but twice. The two brothers sat up and watched their corn all night, and in the morning it was full grown and ripe.

When Kana'ti came home at last, he looked around, but could not see Selu anywhere, and asked the boys where was their mother. "She was a witch, and we killed her," said the boys; "there is her head up there on top of the house." When he saw his wife's head on the roof, he was very angry, and said, "I won't stay with you any longer; I am going to the Wolf people." So he started off, but before he had gone far the Wild Boy changed himself again to a tuft of down, which fell on Kana'ti's shoulder. When Kana'ti reached the settlement of the Wolf people, they were holding a council in the townhouse. He went in and sat down with the tuft of bird's down on his shoulder, but he never noticed it. When the Wolf chief asked him his business, he said: "I have two bad boys at home, and I want you to go in seven days from now and play ball against them." Although Kana'ti spoke as though he wanted them to play a game of ball, the Wolves knew that he meant for them to go and kill the two boys. They promised to go. Then the bird's down blew off from Kana'ti's shoulder, and the smoke carried it up through the hole in the roof of the townhouse. When it came down on the ground outside, the Wild Boy took his right shape again and went home and told his brother all that he had heard in the townhouse. But when Kana'ti left the Wolf people he did not return home, but went on farther.

The boys then began to get ready for the Wolves, and the Wild Boy—the magician—told his brother what to do. They ran around the house in a wide circle until they had made a trail all around it excepting on the side from which the Wolves would come, where they left a small open space. Then they made four large bundles of arrows and placed them at four different points on the outside of the circle, after which they hid themselves in the woods and waited for the Wolves. In a day or two a whole party of Wolves came and surrounded the house to kill the boys. The Wolves did not notice the trail around the house, because they came in where the boys had left the opening, but the moment they went inside the circle the trail changed to a high brush fence and shut them in. Then the boys on the outside took their arrows and began shooting them down, and as the Wolves could not jump over the fence they were all killed, excepting a few that escaped through the opening into a great swamp close by. The boys ran around the swamp, and a circle of fire sprang up in their tracks and set fire to the grass and bushes and burned up nearly all the other Wolves. Only two or three got away, and from these have come all the wolves that are now in the world.

Soon afterward some strangers from a distance, who had heard that the brothers had a wonderful grain from which they made bread, came to ask for some, for none but Selu and her family had ever known corn before. The boys gave them seven grains of corn, which they told them to plant the next night on their way home, sitting up all night to watch the corn, which would have seven ripe ears in the morning. These they were to plant the next night and watch in the same way, and so on every night until they reached home, when they would have corn enough to supply the whole people. The strangers lived seven days' journey away. They took the seven grains and watched all through the darkness until morning, when they saw seven tall stalks, each stalk bearing a ripened ear. They gathered the ears and went on their way. The next night they planted all their corn, and guarded it as before until daybreak, when they found an abundant increase. But the way was long and the sun was hot, and the people grew tired. On the last night before reaching home they fell asleep, and in the morning the corn they had planted had not even sprouted. They brought with them to their settlement what corn they had left and planted it, and with care and attention were able to raise a crop. But ever since the corn must be watched and tended through half the year, which before would grow and ripen in a night.

As Kana'ti did not return, the boys at last concluded to go and find him. The Wild Boy took a gaming wheel and rolled it toward the Darkening land. In a little while the wheel came rolling back, and the boys knew their father was not there. He rolled it to the south and to the north, and each time the wheel came back to him, and they knew their father was not there. Then he rolled it toward the Sunland, and it did not return. "Our father is there," said the Wild Boy, "let us go and find him." So the two brothers set off toward the east, and after traveling a long time they came upon Kana'ti walking along with a little dog by his side. "You bad boys," said their father, "have you come here?" "Yes," they answered, "we always accomplish what we start out to do—we are men." "This dog overtook me four days ago," then said Kana'ti, but the boys knew that the dog was the wheel which they had sent after him to find him. "Well," said Kana'ti, "as you have found me, we may as well travel together, but I shall take the lead."

Soon they came to a swamp, and Kana'ti told them there was something dangerous there and they must keep away from it. He went on ahead, but as soon as he was out of sight the Wild Boy said to his brother, "Come and let us see what is in the swamp." They went in together, and in the middle of the swamp they found a large panther asleep. The Wild Boy got out an arrow and shot the panther in the side of the head. The panther turned his head and the other boy shot him on that side. He turned his head away again and the two brothers shot together—tust, tust, tust! But the panther was not hurt by the arrows and paid no more attention to the boys. They came out of the swamp and soon overtook Kana'ti, waiting for them. "Did you find it?" asked Kana'ti. "Yes," said the boys, "we found it, but it never hurt us. We are men." Kana'ti was surprised, but said nothing, and they went on again.

After a while he turned to them and said, "Now you must be careful. We are coming to a tribe called the Anada'dûñtaski ("Roasters," i. e., cannibals), and if they get you they will put you into a pot and feast on you." Then he went on ahead. Soon the boys came to a tree which had been struck by lightning, and the Wild Boy directed his brother to gather some of the splinters from the tree and told him what to do with them. In a little while they came to the settlement of the cannibals, who, as soon as they saw the boys, came running out, crying, "Good, here are two nice fat strangers. Now we'll have a grand feast!" They caught the boys and dragged them into the townhouse, and sent word to all the people of the settlement to come to the feast. They made up a great fire, put water into a large pot and set it to boiling, and then seized the Wild Boy and put him down into it. His brother was not in the least frightened and made no attempt to escape, but quietly knelt down and began putting the splinters into the fire, as if to make it burn better. When the cannibals thought the meat was about ready they lifted the pot from the fire, and that instant a blinding light filled the townhouse, and the lightning began to dart from one side to the other, striking down the cannibals until not one of them was left alive. Then the lightning went up through the smoke-hole, and the next moment there were the two boys standing outside the townhouse as though nothing had happened. They went on and soon met Kana'ti, who seemed much surprised to see them, and said, "What! are you here again?" "O, yes, we never give up. We are great men!" "What did the cannibals do to you?" "We met them and they brought us to their townhouse, but they never hurt us." Kana'ti said nothing more, and they went on.

He soon got out of sight of the boys, but they kept on until they came to the end of the world, where the sun comes out. The sky was just coming down when they got there, but they waited until it went up again, and then they went through and climbed up on the other side. There they found Kana'ti and Selu sitting together. The old folk received them kindly and were glad to see them, telling them they might stay there a while, but then they must go to live where the sun goes down. The boys stayed with their parents seven days and then went on toward the Darkening land, where they are now. We call them Anisga'ya Tsunsdi' (The Little Men), and when they talk to each other we hear low rolling thunder in the west.

After Kana'ti's boys had let the deer out from the cave where their father used to keep them, the hunters tramped about in the woods for a long time without finding any game, so that the people were very hungry. At last they heard that the Thunder Boys were now living in the far west, beyond the sun door, and that if they were sent for they could bring back the game. So they sent messengers for them, and the boys came and sat down in the middle of the townhouse and began to sing.

At the first song there was a roaring sound like a strong wind in the northwest, and it grew louder and nearer as the boys sang on, until at the seventh song a whole herd of deer, led by a large buck, came out from the woods. The boys had told the people to be ready with their bows and arrows, and when the song was ended and all the deer were close around the townhouse, the hunters shot into them and killed as many as they needed before the herd could get back into the timber.

Then the Thunder Boys went back to the Darkening land, but before they left they taught the people the seven songs with which to call up the deer. It all happened so long ago that the songs are now forgotten—all but two, which the hunters still sing whenever they go after deer.

ORIGIN OF DISEASE AND MEDICINE

In the old days the beasts, birds, fishes, insects, and plants could all talk, and they and the people lived together in peace and friendship. But as time went on the people increased so rapidly that their settlements spread over the whole earth, and the poor animals found themselves beginning to be cramped for room. This was bad enough, but to make it worse Man invented bows, knives, blowguns, spears, and hooks, and began to slaughter the larger animals, birds, and fishes for their flesh or their skins, while the smaller creatures, such as the frogs and worms, were crushed and trodden upon without thought, out of pure carelessness or contempt. So the animals resolved to consult upon measures for their common safety.

The Bears were the first to meet in council in their townhouse under Kuwâ'hi mountain, the "Mulberry place," and the old White Bear chief presided. After each in turn had complained of the way in which Man killed their friends, ate their flesh, and used their skins for his own purposes, it was decided to begin war at once against him. Some one asked what weapons Man used to destroy them. "Bows and arrows, of course," cried all the Bears in chorus. "And what are they made of?" was the next question. "The bow of wood, and the string of our entrails," replied one of the Bears. It was then proposed that they make a bow and some arrows and see if they could not use the same weapons against Man himself. So one Bear got a nice piece of locust wood and another sacrificed himself for the good of the rest in order to furnish a piece of his entrails for the string. But when everything was ready and the first Bear stepped up to make the trial, it was found that in letting the arrow fly after drawing back the bow, his long claws caught the string and spoiled the shot. This was annoying, but some one suggested that they might trim his claws, which was accordingly done, and on a second trial it was found that the arrow went straight to the mark. But here the chief, the old White Bear, objected, saying it was necessary that they should have long claws in order to be able to climb trees. "One of us has already died to furnish the bow-string, and if we now cut off our claws we must all starve together. It is better to trust to the teeth and claws that nature gave us, for it is plain that man's weapons were not intended for us."

No one could think of any better plan, so the old chief dismissed the council and the Bears dispersed to the woods and thickets without having concerted any way to prevent the increase of the human race. Had the result of the council been otherwise, we should now be at war with the Bears, but as it is, the hunter does not even ask the Bear's pardon when he kills one.

The Deer next held a council under their chief, the Little Deer, and after some talk decided to send rheumatism to every hunter who should kill one of them unless he took care to ask their pardon for the offense. They sent notice of their decision to the nearest settlement of Indians and told them at the same time what to do when necessity forced them to kill one of the Deer tribe. Now, whenever the hunter shoots a Deer, the Little Deer, who is swift as the wind and can not be wounded, runs quickly up to the spot and, bending over the blood-stains, asks the spirit of the Deer if it has heard the prayer of the hunter for pardon. If the reply be "Yes," all is well, and the Little Deer goes on his way; but if the reply be "No," he follows on the trail of the hunter, guided by the drops of blood on the ground, until he arrives at his cabin in the settlement, when the Little Deer enters invisibly and strikes the hunter with rheumatism, so that he becomes at once a helpless cripple. No hunter who has regard for his health ever fails to ask pardon of the Deer for killing it, although some hunters who have not learned the prayer may try to turn aside the Little Deer from his pursuit by building a fire behind them in the trail.

Next came the Fishes and Reptiles, who had their own complaints against Man. They held their council together and determined to make their victims dream of snakes twining about them in slimy folds and blowing foul breath in their faces, or to make them dream of eating raw or decaying fish, so that they would lose appetite, sicken, and die. This is why people dream about snakes and fish.

Finally the Birds, Insects, and smaller animals came together for the same purpose, and the Grubworm was chief of the council. It was decided that each in turn should give an opinion, and then they would vote on the question as to whether or not Man was guilty. Seven votes should be enough to condemn him. One after another denounced Man's cruelty and injustice toward the other animals and voted in favor of his death. The Frog spoke first, saying: "We must do something to check the increase of the race, or people will become so numerous that we shall be crowded from off the earth. See how they have kicked me about because I'm ugly, as they say, until my back is covered with sores;" and here he showed the spots on his skin. Next came the Bird—no one remembers now which one it was—who condemned Man "because he burns my feet off," meaning the way in which the hunter barbecues birds by impaling them on a stick set over the fire, so that their feathers and tender feet are singed off. Others followed in the same strain. The Ground-squirrel alone ventured to say a good word for Man, who seldom hurt him because he was so small, but this made the others so angry that they fell upon the Ground-squirrel and tore him with their claws, and the stripes are on his back to this day.

They began then to devise and name so many new diseases, one after another, that had not their invention at last failed them, no one of the human race would have been able to survive. The Grubworm grew constantly more pleased as the name of each disease was called off, until at last they reached the end of the list, when some one proposed to make menstruation sometimes fatal to women. On this he rose up in his place and cried: "Wadâñ'! [Thanks!] I'm glad some more of them will die, for they are getting so thick that they tread on me." The thought fairly made him shake with joy, so that he fell over backward and could not get on his feet again, but had to wriggle off on his back, as the Grubworm has done ever since.

When the Plants, who were friendly to Man, heard what had been done by the animals, they determined to defeat the latters' evil designs. Each Tree, Shrub, and Herb, down even to the Grasses and Mosses, agreed to furnish a cure for some one of the diseases named, and each said: "I shall appear to help Man when he calls upon me in his need." Thus came medicine; and the plants, every one of which has its use if we only knew it, furnish the remedy to counteract the evil wrought by the revengeful animals. Even weeds were made for some good purpose, which we must find out for ourselves. When the doctor does not know what medicine to use for a sick man the spirit of the plant tells him.

THE DAUGHTER OF THE SUN

The Sun lived on the other side of the sky vault, but her daughter lived in the middle of the sky, directly above the earth, and every day as the Sun was climbing along the sky arch to the west she used to stop at her daughter's house for dinner.

Now, the Sun hated the people on the earth, because they could never look straight at her without screwing up their faces. She said to her brother, the Moon, "My grandchildren are ugly; they grin all over their faces when they look at me." But the Moon said, "I like my younger brothers; I think they are very handsome"—because they always smiled pleasantly when they saw him in the sky at night, for his rays were milder.

The Sun was jealous and planned to kill all the people, so every day when she got near her daughter's house she sent down such sultry rays that there was a great fever and the people died by hundreds, until everyone had lost some friend and there was fear that no one would be left. They went for help to the Little Men, who said the only way to save themselves was to kill the Sun.

The Little Men made medicine and changed two men to snakes, the Spreading-adder and the Copperhead, and sent them to watch near the door of the daughter of the Sun to bite the old Sun when she came next day. They went together and hid near the house until the Sun came, but when the Spreading-adder was about to spring, the bright light blinded him and he could only spit out yellow slime, as he does to this day when he tries to bite. She called him a nasty thing and went by into the house, and the Copperhead crawled off without trying to do anything.

So the people still died from the heat, and they went to the Little Men a second time for help. The Little Men made medicine again and changed one man into the great Uktena and another into the Rattlesnake and sent them to watch near the house and kill the old Sun when she came for dinner. They made the Uktena very large, with horns on his head, and everyone thought he would be sure to do the work, but the Rattlesnake was so quick and eager that he got ahead and coiled up just outside the house, and when the Sun's daughter opened the door to look out for her mother, he sprang up and bit her and she fell dead in the doorway. He forgot to wait for the old Sun, but went back to the people, and the Uktena was so very angry that he went back, too. Since then we pray to the rattlesnake and do not kill him, because he is kind and never tries to bite if we do not disturb him. The Uktena grew angrier all the time and very dangerous, so that if he even looked at a man, that man's family would die. After a long time the people held a council and decided that he was too dangerous to be with them, so they sent him up to Galûñ'lati, and he is there now. The Spreading-adder, the Copperhead, the Rattlesnake, and the Uktena were all men.

When the Sun found her daughter dead, she went into the house and grieved, and the people did not die any more, but now the world was dark all the time, because the Sun would not come out. They went again to the Little Men, and these told them that if they wanted the Sun to come out again they must bring back her daughter from Tsûsginâ'i, the Ghost country, in Usûñhi'yi, the Darkening land in the west. They chose seven men to go, and gave each a sourwood rod a hand-breadth long. The Little Men told them they must take a box with them, and when they got to Tsûsginâ'i they would find all the ghosts at a dance. They must stand outside the circle, and when the young woman passed in the dance they must strike her with the rods and she would fall to the ground. Then they must put her into the box and bring her back to her mother, but they must be very sure not to open the box, even a little way, until they were home again.

They took the rods and a box and traveled seven days to the west until they came to the Darkening land. There were a great many people there, and they were having a dance just as if they were at home in the settlements. The young woman was in the outside circle, and as she swung around to where the seven men were standing, one struck her with his rod and she turned her head and saw him. As she came around the second time another touched her with his rod, and then another and another, until at the seventh round she fell out of the ring, and they put her into the box and closed the lid fast. The other ghosts seemed never to notice what had happened.

They took up the box and started home toward the east. In a little while the girl came to life again and begged to be let out of the box, but they made no answer and went on. Soon she called again and said she was hungry, but still they made no answer and went on. After another while she spoke again and called for a drink and pleaded so that it was very hard to listen to her, but the men who carried the box said nothing and still went on. When at last they were very near home, she called again and begged them to raise the lid just a little, because she was smothering. They were afraid she was really dying now, so they lifted the lid a little to give her air, but as they did so there was a fluttering sound inside and something flew past them into the thicket and they heard a redbird cry, "kwish! kwish! kwish!" in the bushes. They shut down the lid and went on again to the settlements, but when they got there and opened the box it was empty.

So we know the Redbird is the daughter of the Sun, and if the men had kept the box closed, as the Little Men told them to do, they would have brought her home safely, and we could bring back our other friends also from the Ghost country, but now when they die we can never bring them back.

The Sun had been glad when they started to the Ghost country, but when they came back without her daughter she grieved and cried, "My daughter, my daughter," and wept until her tears made a flood upon the earth, and the people were afraid the world would be drowned. They held another council, and sent their handsomest young men and women to amuse her so that she would stop crying. They danced before the Sun and sang their best songs, but for a long time she kept her face covered and paid no attention, until at last the drummer suddenly changed the song, when she lifted up her face, and was so pleased at the sight that she forgot her grief and smiled.

THE JOURNEY TO THE SUNRISE

A long time ago several young men made up their minds to find the place where the Sun lives and see what the Sun is like. They got ready their bows and arrows, their parched corn and extra moccasins, and started out toward the east. At first they met tribes they knew, then they came to tribes they had only heard about, and at last to others of which they had never heard.

There was a tribe of root eaters and another of acorn eaters, with great piles of acorn shells near their houses. In one tribe they found a sick man dying, and were told it was the custom there when a man died to bury his wife in the same grave with him. They waited until he was dead, when they saw his friends lower the body into a great pit, so deep and dark that from the top they could not see the bottom. Then a rope was tied around the woman's body, together with a bundle of pine knots, a lighted pine knot was put into her hand, and she was lowered into the pit to die there in the darkness after the last pine knot was burned.

The young men travelled on until they came at last to the sunrise place where the sky reaches down to the ground. They found that the sky was an arch or vault of solid rock hung above the earth and was always swinging up and down, so that when it went up there was an open place like a door between the sky and ground, and when it swung back the door was shut. The Sun came out of this door from the east and climbed along on the inside of the arch. It had a human figure, but was too bright for them to see clearly and too hot to come very near. They waited until the Sun had come out and then tried to get through while the door was still open, but just as the first one was in the doorway the rock came down and crushed him. The other six were afraid to try it, and as they were now at the end of the world they turned around and started back again, but they had travelled so far that they were old men when they reached home.

WHAT THE STARS ARE LIKE

There are different opinions about the stars. Some say they are balls of light, others say they are human, but most people say they are living creatures covered with luminous fur or feathers.

One night a hunting party camping in the mountains noticed two lights like large stars moving along the top of a distant ridge. They wondered and watched until the light disappeared on the other side. The next night, and the next, they saw the lights again moving along the ridge, and after talking over the matter decided to go on the morrow and try to learn the cause. In the morning they started out and went until they came to the ridge, where, after searching some time, they found two strange creatures about so large (making a circle with outstretched arms), with round bodies covered with fine fur or downy feathers, from which small heads stuck out like the heads of terrapins. As the breeze played upon these feathers showers of sparks flew out.

The hunters carried the strange creatures back to the camp, intending to take them home to the settlements on their return. They kept them several days and noticed that every night they would grow bright and shine like great stars, although by day they were only balls of gray fur, except when the wind stirred and made the sparks fly out. They kept very quiet, and no one thought of their trying to escape, when, on the seventh night, they suddenly rose from the ground like balls of fire and were soon above the tops of the trees. Higher and higher they went, while the wondering hunters watched, until at last they were only two bright points of light in the dark sky, and then the hunters knew that they were stars.

THE MILKY WAY

Some people in the south had a corn mill, in which they pounded the corn into meal, and several mornings when they came to fill it they noticed that some of the meal had been stolen during the night. They examined the ground and found the tracks of a dog, so the next night they watched, and when the dog came from the north and began to eat the meal out of the bowl they sprang out and whipped him. He ran off howling to his home in the north, with the meal dropping from his mouth as he ran, and leaving behind a white trail where now we see the Milky Way, which the Cherokee call to this day Gi li' ut sun stan un yi, "the place where the dog ran."

ORIGIN OF STRAWBERRIES

When the first man was created and a mate was given to him, they lived together very happily for a time, but then began to quarrel, until at last the woman left her husband and started off toward Nundagunyi, the Sun land, in the east. The man followed alone and grieving, but the woman kept on steadily ahead and never looked behind, until Unelanunhi, the great Apportioner (the Sun), took pity on him and asked him if he was still angry with his wife. He said he was not, and Unelanunhi then asked him if he would like to have her back again, to which he eagerly answered yes.

So Unelanunhi caused a patch of the finest ripe huckleberries to spring up along the path in front of the woman, but she passed by without paying any attention to them. Farther on he put a clump of blackberries, but these also she refused to notice. Other fruits, one, two, and three, and then some trees covered with beautiful red service berries, were placed beside the path to tempt her, but she still went on until suddenly she saw in front a patch of large ripe strawberries, the first ever known. She stooped to gather a few to eat, and as she picked them she chanced to turn her face to the west, and at once the memory of her husband came back to her and she found herself unable to go on. She sat down, but the longer she waited the stronger became her desire for her husband, and at last she gathered a bunch of the finest berries and started back along the path to give them to him. He met her kindly and they went home together.

THE GREAT YELLOW-JACKET: ORIGIN OF FISH AND FROGS

A long time ago the people of the old town of Kanugalayi ("Brier place," or Briertown), on Nantahala river, in the present Macon county, North Carolina, were much annoyed by a great insect called Ulagu, as large as a house, which used to come from some secret hiding place, and darting swiftly through the air, would snap up children from their play and carry them away. It was unlike any other insect ever known, and the people tried many times to track it to its home, but it was too swift to be followed.

They killed a squirrel and tied a white string to it, so that its course could be followed with the eye, as bee hunters follow the flight of a bee to its tree. The Ulagu came and carried off the squirrel with the string hanging to it, but darted away so swiftly through the air that it was out of sight in a moment. They killed a turkey and put a longer white string to it, and the Ulagu came and took the turkey, but was gone again before they could see in what direction it flew. They took a deer ham and tied a white string to it, and again the Ulagu swooped down and bore it off so swiftly that it could not be followed. At last they killed a yearling deer and tied a very long white string to it. The Ulagu came again and seized the deer, but this time the load was so heavy that it had to fly slowly and so low down that the string could be plainly seen.

The hunters got together for the pursuit. They followed it along a ridge to the east until they came near where Franklin now is, when, on looking across the valley to the other side, they saw the nest of the Ulagu in a large cave in the rocks.

On this they raised a great shout and made their way rapidly down the mountain and across to the cave. The nest had the entrance below with tiers of cells built up one above another to the roof of the cave. The great Ulagu was there, with thousands of smaller ones, that we now call yellow-jackets. The hunters built fires around the hole, so that the smoke filled the cave and smothered the great insect and multitudes of the smaller ones, but others which were outside the cave were not killed, and these escaped and increased until now the yellow-jackets, which before were unknown, are all over the world. The people called the cave Tsgagunyi, "Where the yellow-jacket was," and the place from which they first saw the nest they called Atahita, "Where they shouted," and these are their names today.

They say also that all the fish and frogs came from a great monster fish and frog which did much damage until at last they were killed by the people, who cut them up into little pieces which were thrown into the water and afterward took shape as the smaller fishes and frogs.

THE DELUGE

A long time ago a man had a dog, which began to go down to the river every day and look at the water and howl. At last the man was angry and scolded the dog, which then spoke to him and said: "Very soon there is going to be a great freshet and the water will come so high that everybody will be drowned; but if you will make a raft to get upon when the rain comes you can be saved, but you must first throw me into the water." The man did not believe it, and the dog said, "If you want a sign that I speak the truth, look at the back of my neck." He looked and saw that the dog's neck had the skin worn off so that the bones stuck out.

Then he believed the dog, and began to build a raft. Soon the rain came and he took his family, with plenty of provisions, and they all got upon it. It rained for a long time, and the water rose until the mountains were covered and all the people in the world were drowned. Then the rain stopped and the waters went down again, until at last it was safe to come off the raft. Now there was no one alive but the man and his family, but one day they heard a sound of dancing and shouting on the other side of the ridge. The man climbed to the top and looked over; everything was still, but all along the valley he saw great piles of bones of the people who had been drowned, and then he knew that the ghosts had been dancing.

THE RABBIT GOES DUCK HUNTING

The Rabbit was so boastful that he would claim to do whatever he saw anyone else do, and so tricky that he could usually make the other animals believe it all. Once he pretended that he could swim in the water and eat fish just as the Otter did, and when the others told him to prove it he fixed up a plan so that the Otter himself was deceived.

Soon afterward they met again and the Otter said, "I eat ducks sometimes." Said the Rabbit, "Well, I eat ducks too." The Otter challenged him to try it; so they went up along the river until they saw several ducks in the water and managed to get near without being seen. The Rabbit told the Otter to go first. The Otter never hesitated, but dived from the bank and swam under water until he reached the ducks, when he pulled one down without being noticed by the others, and came back in the same way.

While the Otter had been under the water the Rabbit had peeled some bark from a sapling and made himself a noose. "Now," he said, "Just watch me;" and he dived in and swam a little way under the water until he was nearly choking and had to come up to the top to breathe. He went under again and came up again a little nearer to the ducks. He took another breath and dived under, and this time he came up among the ducks and threw the noose over the head of one and caught it. The duck struggled hard and finally spread its wings and flew up from the water with the Rabbit hanging on to the noose.

It flew on and on until at last the Rabbit could not hold on any longer, but had to let go and drop. As it happened, he fell into a tall, hollow sycamore stump without any hole at the bottom to get out from, and there he stayed until he was so hungry that he had to eat his own fur, as the rabbit does ever since when he is starving. After several days, when he was very weak with hunger, he heard children playing outside around the trees. He began to sing:

> *Cut a door and look at me;*
> *I'm the prettiest thing you ever did see.*

The children ran home and told their father, who came and began to cut a hole in the tree. As he chopped away the Rabbit inside kept singing, "Cut it larger, so you can see me better; I'm so pretty." They made the hole larger, and then the Rabbit told them to stand back so that they could take a good look as he came out. They stood away back, and the Rabbit watched his chance and jumped out and got away.

HOW THE RABBIT STOLE
THE OTTER'S COAT

The animals were of different sizes and wore coats of various colors and patterns. Some wore long fur and others wore short. Some had rings on their tails, and some had no tails at all. Some had coats of brown, others of black or yellow. They were always disputing about their good looks, so at last they agreed to hold a council to decide who had the finest coat.

They had heard a great deal about the Otter, who lived so far up the creek that he seldom came down to visit the other animals. It was said that he had the finest coat of all, but no one knew just what it was like, because it was a long time since anyone had seen him. They did not even know exactly where he lived—only the general direction; but they knew he would come to the council when the word got out.

Now the Rabbit wanted the verdict for himself, so when it began to look as if it might go to the Otter he studied up a plan to cheat him out of it. He asked a few sly questions until he learned what trail the Otter would take to get to the council place. Then, without saying anything, he went on ahead and after four days' travel he met the Otter and knew him at once by his beautiful coat of soft dark-brown fur. The Otter was glad to see him and asked him where he was going. "O," said the Rabbit, "the animals sent me to bring you to the council; because you live so far away they were afraid you mightn't know the road." The Otter thanked him, and they went on together.

They traveled all day toward the council ground, and at night the Rabbit selected the camping place, because the Otter was a stranger in that part of the country, and cut down bushes for beds and fixed everything in good shape. The next morning they started on again. In the afternoon the Rabbit began to pick up wood and bark as they went along and to load it on his back. When the Otter asked what this was for the Rabbit said it was that they might be warm and comfortable at night. After a while, when it was near sunset, they stopped and made their camp.

When supper was over the Rabbit got a stick and shaved it down to a paddle. The Otter wondered and asked again what that was for.

"I have good dreams when I sleep with a paddle under my head," said the Rabbit.

When the paddle was finished the Rabbit began to cut away the bushes so as to make a clean trail down to the river. The Otter wondered more and more and wanted to know what this meant.

Said the Rabbit, "This place is called Di'tatlâski'yi [The Place Where it Rains Fire]. Sometimes it rains fire here, and the sky looks a little that way to-night. You go to sleep and I'll sit up and watch, and if the fire does come, as soon as you hear me shout, you run and jump into the river. Better hang your coat on a limb over there, so it won't get burnt."

The Otter did as he was told, and they both doubled up to go to sleep, but the Rabbit kept awake. After a while the fire burned down to red coals. The Rabbit called, but the Otter was fast asleep and made no answer. In a little while he called again, but the Otter never stirred. Then the Rabbit filled the paddle with hot coals and threw them up into the air and shouted, "It's raining fire! It's raining fire!"

The hot coals fell all around the Otter and he jumped up. "To the water!" cried the Rabbit, and the Otter ran and jumped into the river, and he has lived in the water ever since.

The Rabbit took the Otter's coat and put it on, leaving his own instead, and went on to the council. All the animals were there, every one looking out for the Otter. At last they saw him in the distance, and they said one to the other, "The Otter is coming!" and sent one of the small animals to show him the best seat. They were all glad to see him and went up in turn to welcome him, but the Otter kept his head down, with one paw over his face. They wondered that he was so bashful, until the Bear came up and pulled the paw away, and there was the Rabbit with his split nose. He sprang up and started to run, when the Bear struck at him and pulled his tail off, but the Rabbit was too quick for them and got away.

WHY THE POSSUM'S TAIL IS BARE

The Possum used to have a long, bushy tail, and was so proud of it that he combed it out every morning and sang about it at the dance, until the Rabbit, who had had no tail since the Bear pulled it out, became very jealous and made up his mind to play the Possum a trick.

There was to be a great council and a dance at which all the animals were to be present. It was the Rabbit's business to send out the news, so as he was passing the Possum's place he stopped to ask him if he intended to be there. The Possum said he would come if he could have a special seat, "because I have such a handsome tail that I ought to sit where everybody can see me." The Rabbit promised to attend to it and to send some one besides to comb and dress the Possum's tail for the dance, so the Possum was very much pleased and agreed to come.

Then the Rabbit went over to the Cricket, who is such an expert hair cutter that the Indians call him the barber, and told him to go next morning and dress the Possum's tail for the dance that night. He told the Cricket just what to do and then went on about some other mischief.

In the morning the Cricket went to the Possum's house and said he had come to get him ready for the dance. So the Possum stretched himself out and shut his eyes while the Cricket combed out his tail and wrapped a red string around it to keep it smooth until night. But all this time, as he wound the string around, he was clipping off the hair close to the roots, and the Possum never knew it.

When it was night the Possum went to the townhouse

where the dance was to be and found the best seat ready for him, just as the Rabbit had promised. When his turn came in the dance he loosened the string from his tail and stepped into the middle of the floor. The drummers began to drum and the Possum began to sing, "See my beautiful tail." Everybody shouted and he danced around the circle and sang again, "See what a fine color it has." They shouted again and he danced around another time, singing, "See how it sweeps the ground." The animals shouted more loudly than ever, and the Possum was delighted. He danced around again and sang, "See how fine the fur is." Then everybody laughed so long that the Possum wondered what they meant. He looked around the circle of animals and they were all laughing at him. Then he looked down at his beautiful tail and saw that there was not a hair left upon it, but that it was as bare as the tail of a lizard. He was so much astonished and ashamed that he could not say a word, but rolled over helpless on the ground and grinned, as the Possum does to this day when taken by surprise.

HOW THE WILDCAT CAUGHT THE GOBBLER

The Wildcat once caught the Rabbit and was about to kill him, when the Rabbit begged for his life, saying: "I'm so small I would make only a mouthful for you, but if you let me go I'll show you where you can get a whole drove of Turkeys." So the Wildcat let him up and went with him to where the Turkeys were.

When they came near the place the Rabbit said to the Wildcat, "Now, you must do just as I say. Lie down as if you were dead and don't move, even if I kick you, but when I give the word jump up and catch the largest one there." The Wildcat agreed and stretched out as if dead, while the Rabbit gathered some rotten wood and crumbled it over his eyes and nose to make them look flyblown, so that the Turkeys would think he had been dead some time.

Then the Rabbit went over to the Turkeys and said, in a sociable way, "Here, I've found our old enemy, the Wildcat, lying dead in the trail. Let's have a dance over him." The Turkeys were very doubtful, but finally went with him to where the Wildcat was lying in the road as if dead. Now, the Rabbit had a good voice and was a great dance leader, so he said, "I'll lead the song and you dance around him." The Turkeys thought that fine, so the Rabbit took a stick to beat time and began to sing: "Galagina hasuyak, Galagina hasuyak (pick out the Gobbler, pick out the Gobbler)."

"Why do you say that?" said the old Turkey. "O, that's all right," said the Rabbit, "that's just the way he does, and we sing about it." He started the song again and the Turkeys began to dance around the Wildcat. When they had gone around several times the Rabbit said, "Now go up and hit him, as we do in the war dance." So the Turkeys, thinking the Wildcat surely dead, crowded in close around him and the old gobbler kicked him. Then the Rabbit drummed hard and sang his loudest, "Pick out the Gobbler, pick out the Gobbler," and the Wildcat jumped up and caught the Gobbler.

HOW THE TERRAPIN BEAT THE RABBIT

The Rabbit was a great runner, and everybody knew it. No one thought the Terrapin anything but a slow traveler, but he was a great warrior and very boastful, and the two were always disputing about their speed. At last they agreed to decide the matter by a race. They fixed the day and the starting place and arranged to run across four mountain ridges, and the one who came in first at the end was to be the winner.

The Rabbit felt so sure of it that he said to the Terrapin, "You know you can't run. You can never win the race, so I'll give you the first ridge and then you'll have only three to cross while I go over four."

The Terrapin said that would be all right, but that night when he went home to his family he sent for his Terrapin friends and told them he wanted their help. He said he knew he could not outrun the Rabbit, but he wanted to stop the Rabbit's boasting. He explained his plan to his friends and they agreed to help him.

When the day came all the animals were there to see the race. The Rabbit was with them, but the Terrapin was gone ahead toward the first ridge, as they had arranged, and they could hardly see him on account of the long grass. The word was given and the Rabbit started off with long jumps up the mountain, expecting to win the race before the Terrapin could get down the other side. But before he got up the mountain he saw the Terrapin go over the ridge ahead of him. He ran on, and when he reached the top he looked all around, but could not see the Terrapin on account of the long grass. He kept on down the mountain and began to climb the second ridge, but when he looked up again there was the Terrapin just going over the top. Now he was surprised and made his longest jumps to catch up, but when he got to the top there was the Terrapin away in front going over the third ridge. The Rabbit was getting tired now and nearly out of breath, but he kept on down the mountain and up the other ridge until he got to the top just in time to see the Terrapin cross the fourth ridge and thus win the race.

The Rabbit could not make another jump, but fell over on the ground, crying mi, mi, mi, mi, as the Rabbit does ever since when he is too tired to run any more. The race was given to the Terrapin and all the animals wondered how he could win against the Rabbit, but he kept still and never told. It was easy enough, however, because all the Terrapin's friends looked just alike, and he had simply posted one near the top of each ridge to wait until the Rabbit came in sight and then climb over and hide in the long grass. When the Rabbit came on he could not find the Terrapin and so thought the Terrapin was ahead, and if he had met one of the other terrapins he would have thought it the same one because they looked so much alike. The real Terrapin had posted himself on the fourth ridge, so as to come in at the end of the race and be ready to answer questions if the animals suspected anything.

Because the Rabbit had to lie down and lose the race the conjurer now, when preparing his young men for the ball play, boils a lot of rabbit hamstrings into a soup, and sends some one at night to pour it across the path along which the other players are to come in the morning, so that they may become tired in the same way and lose the game. It is not always easy to do this, because the other party is expecting it and has watchers ahead to prevent it.

THE RABBIT AND
THE TAR WOLF

Once there was such a long spell of dry weather that there was no more water in the creeks and springs, and the animals held a council to see what to do about it. They decided to dig a well, and all agreed to help except the Rabbit, who was a lazy fellow, and said, "I don't need to dig for water. The dew on the grass is enough for me." The others did not like this, but they went to work together and dug their well.

They noticed that the Rabbit kept sleek and lively, although it was still dry weather and the water was getting low in the well. They said, "That tricky Rabbit steals our water at night," so they made a wolf of pine gum and tar and set it up by the well to scare the thief. That night the Rabbit came, as he had been coming every night, to drink enough to last him all next day. He saw the queer black thing by the well and said, "Who's there?" but the tar wolf said nothing. He came nearer, but the wolf never moved, so he grew braver and said, "Get out of my way or I'll strike you." Still the wolf never moved and the Rabbit came up and struck it with his paw, but the gum held his foot and it stuck fast. Now he was angry and said, "Let me go or I'll kick you." Still the wolf said nothing. Then the Rabbit struck again with his hind foot, so hard that it was caught in the gum and he could not move, and there he stuck until the animals came for water in the morning. When they found who the thief was they had great sport over him for a while and then got ready to kill him, but as soon as he was unfastened from the tar wolf he managed to get away.

THE RABBIT AND THE POSSUM AFTER A WIFE

The Rabbit and the Possum each wanted a wife, but no one would marry either of them. They talked over the matter and the Rabbit said, "We can't get wives here; let's go to the next settlement. I'm the messenger for the council, and I'll tell the people that I bring an order that everybody must take a mate at once, and then we'll be sure to get our wives."

The Possum thought this a fine plan, so they started off together to the next town. As the Rabbit travelled faster he got there first and waited outside until the people noticed him and took him into the townhouse. When the chief came to ask his business the Rabbit said he brought an important order from the council that everybody must get married without delay. So the chief called the people together and told them the message from the council. Every animal took a mate at once, and the Rabbit got a wife.

The Possum travelled so slowly that he got there after all the animals had mated, leaving him still without a wife. The Rabbit pretended to feel sorry for him and said, "Never mind, I'll carry the message to the people in the next settlement, and you hurry on as fast as you can, and this time you will get your wife."

So he went on to the next town, and the Possum followed close after him. But when the Rabbit got to the townhouse he sent out the word that, as there had been peace so long that everybody was getting lazy the council had ordered that there must be war at once and they must begin right in the townhouse. So they all began fighting, but the Rabbit made four great leaps and got away just as the Possum came in.

Everybody jumped on the Possum, who had not thought of bringing his weapons on a wedding trip, and so could not defend himself. They had nearly beaten the life out of him when he fell over and pretended to be dead until he saw a good chance to jump up and get away. The Possum never got a wife, but he remembers the lesson, and ever since he shuts his eyes and pretends to be dead when the hunter has him in a close corner.

THE RABBIT DINES THE BEAR

The Bear invited the Rabbit to dine with him. They had beans in the pot, but there was no grease for them, so the Bear cut a slit in his side and let the oil run out until they had enough to cook the dinner. The Rabbit looked surprised, and thought to himself, "That's a handy way. I think I'll try that." When he started home he invited the Bear to come and take dinner with him four days later.

When the Bear came the Rabbit said, "I have beans for dinner, too. Now I'll get the grease for them." So he took a knife and drove it into his side, but instead of oil, a stream of blood gushed out and he fell over nearly dead. The Bear picked him up and had hard work to tie up the wound and stop the bleeding. Then he scolded him, "You little fool, I'm large and strong and lined with fat all over; the knife don't hurt me; but you're small and lean, and you can't do such things."

THE RABBIT ESCAPES FROM THE WOLVES

Some Wolves once caught the Rabbit and were going to eat him when he asked leave to show them a new dance he was practicing. They knew that the Rabbit was a great song leader, and they wanted to learn the latest dance, so they agreed and made a ring about him while he got ready. He patted his feet and began to dance around in a circle, singing:

> *On the edge of the field I dance about—*
> *Ha'nia lil! lil! Ha'nia lil! lil!*

"Now," said the Rabbit, "when I sing 'on the edge of the field,' I dance that way"—and he danced over in that direction—"and when I sing 'lil! lil!' you must all stamp your feet hard." The Wolves thought it fine. He began another round singing the same song, and danced a little nearer to the field, while the Wolves all stamped their feet. He sang louder and louder and danced nearer and nearer to the field until at the fourth song, when the Wolves were stamping as hard as they could and thinking only of the song, he made one jump and was off through the long grass. They were after him at once, but he ran for a hollow stump and climbed up on the inside. When the the Wolves got there one of them put his head inside to look up, but the Rabbit spit into his eye, so that he had to pull his head out again. The others were afraid to try, and they went away, with the Rabbit still in the stump.

FLINT VISITS THE RABBIT

In the old days Tawi'skala (Flint) lived up in the mountains, and all the animals hated him because he had helped to kill so many of them. They used to get together to talk over means to put him out of the way, but everybody was afraid to venture near his house until the Rabbit, who was the boldest leader among them, offered to go after Flint and try to kill him. They told him where to find him, and the Rabbit set out and at last came to Flint's house.

Flint was standing at his door when the Rabbit came up and said, sneeringly, "Siyu! Hello! Are you the fellow they call Flint?" "Yes; that's what they call me," answered Flint. "Is this where you live?" "Yes; this is where I live." All this time the Rabbit was looking about the place trying to study out some plan to take Flint off his guard. He had expected Flint to invite him into the house, so he waited a little while, but when Flint made no move, he said, "Well, my name is Rabbit; I've heard a good deal about you, so I came to invite you to come and see me."

Flint wanted to know where the Rabbit's house was, and he told him it was down in the broom-grass field near the river. So Flint promised to make him a visit in a few days. "Why not come now and have supper with me?" said the Rabbit, and after a little coaxing Flint agreed and the two started down the mountain together.

When they came near the Rabbit's hole the Rabbit said, "There is my house, but in summer I generally stay outside here where it is cooler." So he made a fire, and they had their supper on the grass. When it was over, Flint stretched out to rest and the Rabbit got some heavy sticks and his knife and cut out a mallet and wedge. Flint looked up and asked what that was for. "Oh," said the Rabbit, "I like to be doing something, and they may come handy." So Flint lay down again, and pretty soon he was sound asleep. The Rabbit spoke to him once or twice to make sure, but there was no answer. Then he came over to Flint and with one good blow of the mallet he drove the sharp stake into his body and ran with all his might for his own hole; but before he reached it there was a loud explosion, and pieces of flint flew all about. That is why we find flint in so many places now. One piece struck the Rabbit from behind and cut him just as he dived into his hole. He sat listening until everything seemed quiet again. Then he put his head out to look around, but just at that moment another piece fell and struck him on the lip and split it, as we still see it.

HOW THE DEER GOT HIS HORNS

In the beginning the Deer had no horns, but his head was smooth just like a doe's. He was a great runner and the Rabbit was a great jumper, and the animals were all curious to know which could go farther in the same time. They talked about it a good deal, and at last arranged a match between the two, and made a nice large pair of antlers for a prize to the winner. They were to start together from one side of a thicket and go through it, then turn and come back, and the one who came out first was to get the horns.

On the day fixed all the animals were there, with the antlers put down on the ground at the edge of the thicket to mark the starting point. While everybody was admiring the horns the Rabbit said: "I don't know this part of the country; I want to take a look through the bushes where I am to run." They thought that all right, so the Rabbit went into the thicket, but he was gone so long that at last the animals suspected he must be up to one of his tricks. They sent a messenger to look for him, and away in the middle of the thicket he found the Rabbit gnawing down the bushes and pulling them away until he had a road cleared nearly to the other side.

The messenger turned around quietly and came back and told the other animals. When the Rabbit came out at last they accused him of cheating, but he denied it until they went into the thicket and found the cleared road. They agreed that such a trickster had no right to enter the race at all, so they gave the horns to the Deer, who was admitted to be the best runner, and he has worn them ever since. They told the Rabbit that as he was so fond of cutting down bushes he might do that for a living hereafter, and so he does to this day.

HOW THE DEER GOT HIS HORNS

WHY THE DEER'S TEETH
ARE BLUNT

The Rabbit felt sore because the Deer had won the horns (see the last story), and resolved to get even. One day soon after the race he stretched a large grapevine across the trail and gnawed it nearly in two in the middle. Then he went back a piece, took a good run, and jumped up at the vine. He kept on running and jumping up at the vine until the Deer came along and asked him what he was doing?

"Don't you see?" says the Rabbit. "I'm so strong that I can bite through that grapevine at one jump."

The Deer could hardly believe this, and wanted to see it done. So the Rabbit ran back, made a tremendous spring, and bit through the vine where he had gnawed it before. The Deer, when he saw that, said, "Well, I can do it if you can." So the Rabbit stretched a larger grapevine across the trail, but without gnawing it in the middle. The Deer ran back as he had seen the Rabbit do, made a spring, and struck the grapevine right in the center, but it only flew back and threw him over on his head. He tried again and again, until he was all bruised and bleeding.

"Let me see your teeth," at last said the Rabbit. So the Deer showed him his teeth, which were long like a wolf's teeth, but not very sharp.

"No wonder you can't do it," says the Rabbit; "your teeth are too blunt to bite anything. Let me sharpen them for you like mine. My teeth are so sharp that I can cut through a stick just like a knife." And he showed him a black locust twig, of which rabbits gnaw the young shoots, which he had shaved off as well as a knife could do it, in regular rabbit fashion.

The Deer thought that just the thing. So the Rabbit got a hard stone with rough edges and filed and filed away at the Deer's teeth until they were worn down almost to the gums.

"It hurts," said the Deer; but the Rabbit said it always hurt a little when they began to get sharp; so the Deer kept quiet.

"Now try it," at last said the Rabbit. So the Deer tried again, but this time he could not bite at all.

"Now you've paid for your horns," said the Rabbit, as he jumped away through the bushes. Ever since then the Deer's teeth are so blunt that he can not chew anything but grass and leaves.

WHAT BECAME OF THE RABBIT

The Deer was very angry at the Rabbit for filing his teeth and determined to be revenged, but he kept still and pretended to be friendly until the Rabbit was off his guard. Then one day, as they were going along together talking, he challenged the Rabbit to jump against him. Now the Rabbit is a great jumper, as every one knows, so he agreed at once. There was a small stream beside the path, as there generally is in that country, and the Deer said:

"Let's see if you can jump across this branch. We'll go back a piece, and then when I say Ku! Then both run and jump."

"All right," said the Rabbit. So they went back to get a good start, and when the Deer gave the word Ku! They ran for the stream, and the Rabbit made one jump and landed on the other side. But the Deer had stopped on the bank, and when the Rabbit looked back the Deer had conjured the stream so that it was a large river. The Rabbit was never able to get back again and is still on the other side. The rabbit that we know is only a little thing that came afterwards.

WHY THE MINK SMELLS

The Mink was such a great thief that at last the animals held a council about the matter. It was decided to burn him, so they caught the Mink, built a great fire, and threw him into it. As the blaze went up and they smelt the roasted flesh, they began to think he was punished enough and would probably do better in the future, so they took him out of the fire. But the Mink was already burned black and is black ever since, and whenever he is attacked or excited he smells again like roasted meat. The lesson did no good, however, and he is still as great a thief as ever.

WHY THE MOLE LIVES UNDERGROUND

A man was in love with a woman who disliked him and would have nothing to do with him. He tried every way to win her favor, but to no purpose, until at last he grew discouraged and made himself sick thinking over it. The Mole came along, and finding him in such low condition asked what was the trouble. The man told him the whole story, and when he had finished the Mole said: "I can help you, so that she will not only like you, but will come to you of her own will." So that night the Mole burrowed his way underground to where the girl was in bed asleep and took out her heart. He came back by the same way and gave the heart to the man, who could not see it even when it was put into his hand. "There," said the Mole, "swallow it, and she will be drawn to come to you and can not keep away." The man swallowed the heart, and when the girl woke up she somehow thought at once of him, and felt a strange desire to be with him, as though she must go to him at once. She wondered and could not understand it, because she had always disliked him before, but at last the feeling grew so strong that she was compelled to go herself to the man and tell him she loved him and wanted to be his wife. And so they were married, but all the magicians who had known them both were surprised and wondered how it had come about. When they found that it was the work of the Mole, whom they had always before thought too insignificant for their notice, they were very jealous and threatened to kill him, so that he hid himself under the ground and has never since dared to come up to the surface.

THE MIGRATION OF
THE ANIMALS

In the old times when the animals used to talk and hold councils, and the Grubworm and Woodchuck used to marry people, there was once a great famine of mast in the mountains, and all the animals and birds which lived upon it met together and sent the Pigeon out to the low country to see if any food could be found there. After a time she came back and reported that she had found a country where the mast was "up to our ankles" on the ground. So they got together and moved down into the low country in a great army.

THE WOLF'S REVENGE—
THE WOLF AND THE DOG

Kanati had wolves to hunt for him, because they are good hunters and never fail. He once sent out two wolves at once. One went to the east and did not return. The other went to the north, and when he returned at night and did not find his fellow he knew he must be in trouble and started after him. After traveling on some time he found his brother lying nearly dead beside a great greensnake (salikwayi) which had attacked him. The snake itself was too badly wounded to crawl away, and the angry wolf, who had magic powers, taking out several hairs from his own whiskers, shot them into the body of the snake and killed it. He then hurried back to Kanati, who sent the Terrapin after a great doctor who lived in the west to save the wounded wolf. The wolf went back to help his brother and by his magic powers he had him cured long before the doctor came from the west, because the Terrapin was such a slow traveller and the doctor had to prepare his roots before he started.

In the beginning, the people say, the Dog was put on the mountain and the Wolf beside the fire. When the winter came the Dog could not stand the cold, so he came down to the settlement and drove the Wolf from the fire. The Wolf ran to the mountains, where it suited him so well that he prospered and increased, until after a while he ventured down again and killed some animals in the settlements. The people got together and followed and killed him, but his brothers came from the mountains and took such revenge that ever since the people have been afraid to hurt a wolf.

HOW THE TURKEY
GOT HIS BEARD

When the Terrapin won the race from the Rabbit (see the story) all the animals wondered and talked about it a great deal, because they had always thought the Terrapin slow, although they knew that he was a warrior and had many conjuring secrets beside. But the Turkey was not satisfied and told the others there must be some trick about it. Said he, "I know the Terrapin can't run—he can hardly crawl—and I'm going to try him."

So one day the Turkey met the Terrapin coming home from war with a fresh scalp hanging from his neck and dragging on the ground as he travelled. The Turkey laughed at the sight and said: "That scalp don't look right on you. Your neck is too short and low down to wear it that way. Let me show you."

The Terrapin agreed and gave the scalp to the Turkey, who fastened it around his neck. "Now," said the Turkey, "I'll walk a little way and you can see how it looks." So he walked ahead a short distance and then turned and asked the Terrapin how he liked it. Said the Terrapin, "It looks very nice; it becomes you."

"Now I'll fix it in a different way and let you see how it looks," said the Turkey. So he gave the string another pull and walked ahead again. "O, that looks very nice," said the Terrapin. But the Turkey kept on walking, and when the Terrapin called to him to bring back the scalp he only walked faster and broke into a run. Then the Terrapin got out his bow and by his conjuring art shot a number of cane splints into the Turkey's leg to cripple him so that he could not run, which accounts for all the many small bones in the Turkey's leg, that are of no use whatever; but the Terrapin never caught the Turkey, who still wears the scalp from his neck.

WHY THE TURKEY GOBBLES

The Grouse used to have a fine voice and a good halloo in the ballplay. All the animals and birds used to play ball in those days and were just as proud of a loud halloo as the ball players of today. The Turkey had not a good voice, so he asked the Grouse to give him lessons. The Grouse agreed to teach him, but wanted pay for his trouble, and the Turkey promised to give him some feathers to make himself a collar. That is how the Grouse got his collar of turkey feathers. They began the lessons and the Turkey learned very fast until the Grouse thought it was time to try his voice. "Now," said the Grouse, "I'll stand on this hollow log, and when I give the signal by tapping on it, you must halloo as loudly as you can." So he got upon the log ready to tap on it, as a Grouse does, but when he gave the signal the Turkey was so eager and excited that he could not raise his voice for a shout, but only gobbled, and ever since then he gobbles whenever he hears a noise.

HOW THE KINGFISHER
GOT HIS BILL

Some old men say that the Kingfisher was meant in the beginning to be a water bird, but as he had not been given either web feet or a good bill he could not make a living. The animals held a council over it and decided to make him a bill like a long sharp awl for a fish-gig (fish-spear). So they made him a fish-gig and fastened it on in front of his mouth. He flew to the top of a tree, sailed out and darted down into the water, and came up with a fish on his gig. And he has been the best gigger ever since.

Some others say it was this way: A Blacksnake found a Yellowhammer's nest in a hollow tree, and after swallowing the young birds, coiled up to sleep in the nest, where the mother bird found him when she came home. She went for help to the Little People, who sent her to the Kingfisher. He came, and after flying back and forth past the hole a few times, made one dart at the snake and pulled him out dead. When they looked they found a hole in the snake's head where the Kingfisher had pierced it with a slender tugaluna fish, which he carried in his bill like a lance. From this the Little People concluded that he would make a first-class gigger if he only had the right spear, so they gave him his long bill as a reward.

HOW THE PARTRIDGE
GOT HIS WHISTLE

In the old days the Terrapin had a fine whistle, but the Partridge had none. The Terrapin was constantly going about whistling and showing his whistle to the other animals until the Partridge became jealous, so one day when they met the Partridge asked leave to try it. The Terrapin was afraid to risk it at first, suspecting some trick, but the Partridge said, "I'll give it back right away, and if you are afraid you can stay with me while I practice." So the Terrapin let him have the whistle and the Partridge walked around blowing on it in fine fashion. "How does it sound with me?" asked the Partridge. "O, you do very well," said the Terrapin, walking alongside. "Now, how do you like it," said the Partridge, running ahead and whistling a little faster. "That's fine," answered the Terrapin, hurrying to keep up, "but don't run so fast." "And now, how do you like this?" called the Partridge, and with that he spread his wings, gave one long whistle, and flew to the top of a tree, leaving the poor Terrapin to look after him from the ground. The Terrapin never recovered his whistle, and from that, and the loss of his scalp, which the Turkey stole from him, he grew ashamed to be seen, and ever since he shuts himself up in his box when anyone comes near him.

HOW THE REDBIRD
GOT HIS COLOR

A Raccoon passing a Wolf one day made several insulting remarks, until at last the Wolf became angry and turned and chased him. The Raccoon ran his best and managed to reach a tree by the river side before the Wolf came up. He climbed the tree and stretched out on a limb overhanging the water. When the Wolf arrived he saw the reflection in the water, and thinking it was the Raccoon he jumped at it and was nearly drowned before he could scramble out again, all wet and dripping. He lay down on the bank to dry and fell asleep, and while he was sleeping the Raccoon came down the tree and plastered his eyes with dung. When the Wolf awoke he found he could not open his eyes, and began to whine. Along came a little brown bird through the bushes and heard the Wolf crying and asked what was the matter. The Wolf told his story and said, "If you will get my eyes open, I will show you where to find some nice red paint to paint yourself." "All right," said the brown bird; so he pecked at the Wolf's eyes until he got off all the plaster. Then the Wolf took him to a rock that had streaks of bright red paint running through it, and the little bird painted himself with it, and has ever since been a Redbird.

THE PHEASANT BEATING CORN; ORIGIN OF THE PHEASANT DANCE

The Pheasant once saw a woman beating corn in a wooden mortar in front of the house. "I can do that, too," said he, but the woman would not believe it, so the Pheasant went into the woods and got upon a hollow log and "drummed" with his wings as a pheasant does, until the people in the house heard him and thought he was really beating corn.

In the Pheasant dance, a part of the Green-corn dance, the instrument used is the drum, and the dancers beat the ground with their feet in imitation of the drumming sound made by the pheasant. They form two concentric circles, the men being on the inside, facing the women in the outer circle, each in turn advancing and retreating at the signal of the drummer, who sits at one side and sings the Pheasant songs. According to the story, there was once a winter famine among the birds and animals. No mast (fallen nuts) could be found in the woods, and they were near starvation when a Pheasant discovered a holly tree, loaded with red berries, of which the Pheasant is said to be particularly fond. He called his companion birds, and they formed a circle about the tree, singing, dancing, and drumming with their wings in token of their joy, and thus originated the Pheasant dance.

THE RACE BETWEEN
THE CRANE AND THE
HUMMINGBIRD

The Hummingbird and the Crane were both in love with a pretty woman. She preferred the Hummingbird, who was as handsome as the Crane was awkward, but the Crane was so persistent that in order to get rid of him she finally told him he must challenge the other to a race and she would marry the winner. The Hummingbird was so swift—almost like a flash of lightning—and the Crane so slow and heavy, that she felt sure the Hummingbird would win. She did not know the Crane could fly all night.

They agreed to start from her house and fly around the circle of the world to the beginning, and the one who came in first would marry the woman. At the word the Hummingbird darted off like an arrow and was out of sight in a moment, leaving his rival to follow heavily behind. He flew all day, and when evening came and he stopped to roost for the night he was far ahead. But the Crane flew steadily all night long, passing the Hummingbird soon after midnight and going on until he came to a creek and stopped to rest about daylight. The Hummingbird woke up in the morning and flew on again, thinking how easily he would win the race, until he reached the creek and there found the Crane spearing tadpoles, with his long bill, for breakfast. He was very much surprised and wondered how this could have happened, but he flew swiftly by and soon left the Crane out of sight again.

The Crane finished his breakfast and started on, and when evening came he kept on as before. This time it was hardly midnight when he passed the Hummingbird asleep on a limb, and in the morning he had finished his breakfast before the other came up. The next day he gained a little more, and on the fourth day he was spearing tadpoles for dinner when the Hummingbird passed him. On the fifth and sixth days it was late in the afternoon before the Hummingbird came up, and on the morning of the seventh day the Crane was a whole night's travel ahead. He took his time at breakfast and then fixed himself up as nicely as he could at the creek and came in at the starting place where the woman lived, early in the morning. When the Hummingbird arrived in the afternoon he found he had lost the race, but the woman declared she would never have such an ugly fellow as the Crane for a husband, so she stayed single.

THE OWL GETS MARRIED

A widow with one daughter was always warning the girl that she must be sure to get a good hunter for a husband when she married. The young woman listened and promised to do as her mother advised. At last a suitor came to ask the mother for the girl, but the widow told him that only a good hunter could have her daughter. "I'm just that kind," said the lover, and again asked her to speak for him to the young woman. So the mother went to the girl and told her a young man had come a-courting, and as he said he was a good hunter she advised her daughter to take him. "Just as you say," said the girl. So when he came again the matter was all arranged, and he went to live with the girl.

The next morning he got ready and said he would go out hunting, but before starting he changed his mind and said he would go fishing. He was gone all day and came home late at night, bringing only three small fish, saying that he had had no luck, but would have better success to-morrow. The next morning he started off again to fish and was gone all day, but came home at night with only two worthless spring lizards (duwega) and the same excuse. Next day he said he would go hunting this time. He was gone again until night, and returned at last with only a handful of scraps that he had found where some hunters had cut up a deer.

By this time the old woman was suspicious. So next morning when he started off again, as he said, to fish, she told her daughter to follow him secretly and see how he set to work. The girl followed through the woods and kept him in sight until he came down to the river, where she saw her husband change to a hooting owl (uguku) and fly over to a pile

- 117 -

of driftwood in the water and cry, "U-gu-ku! hu! hu! u! u!" She was surprised and very angry and said to herself, "I thought I had married a man, but my husband is only an owl." She watched and saw the owl look into the water for a long time and at last swoop down and bring up in his claws a handful of sand, from which he picked out a crawfish. Then he flew across to the bank, took the form of a man again, and started home with the crawfish. His wife hurried on ahead through the woods and got there before him. When he came in with the crawfish in his hand, she asked him where were all the fish he had caught. He said he had none, because an owl had frightened them all away. "I think you are the owl," said his wife, and drove him out of the house. The owl went into the woods and there he pined away with grief and love until there was no flesh left on any part of his body except his head.

WHY THE BUZZARD'S HEAD IS BARE

The buzzard used to have a fine topknot, of which he was so proud that he refused to eat carrion, and while the other birds were pecking at the body of a deer or other animal which they had found he would strut around and say: "You may have it all, it is not good enough for me." They resolved to punish him, and with the help of the buffalo carried out a plot by which the buzzard lost not his topknot alone, but nearly all the other feathers on his head. He lost his pride at the same time, so that he is willing enough now to eat carrion for a living.

THE EAGLE'S REVENGE

Once a hunter in the mountains heard a noise at night like a rushing wind outside the cabin, and on going out he found that an eagle had just alighted on the drying pole and was tearing at the body of a deer hanging there. Without thinking of the danger, he shot the eagle. In the morning he took the deer and started back to the settlement, where he told what he had done, and the chief sent out some men to bring in the eagle and arrange for an Eagle dance. They brought back the dead eagle, everything was made ready, and that night they started the dance in the townhouse.

About midnight there was a whoop outside and a strange warrior came into the circle and began to recite his exploits. No one knew him, but they thought he had come from one of the farther Cherokee towns. He told how he had killed a man, and at the end of the story he gave a hoarse yell, Hi! that startled the whole company, and one of the seven men with the rattles fell over dead. He sang of another deed, and at the end straightened up with another loud yell. A second rattler fell dead, and the people were so full of fear that they could not stir from their places. Still he kept on, and at every pause there came again that terrible scream, until the last of the seven rattlers fell dead, and then the stranger went out into the darkness. Long afterward they learned from the eagle killer that it was the brother of the eagle shot by the hunter.

THE HUNTER AND
THE BUZZARD

A hunter had been all day looking for deer in the mountains without success until he was completely tired out and sat down on a log to rest and wonder what he should do, when a buzzard—a bird which always has magic powers—came flying overhead and spoke to him, asking him what was his trouble. When the hunter had told his story the buzzard said there were plenty of deer on the ridges beyond if only the hunter were high up in the air where he could see them, and proposed that they exchange forms for a while, when the buzzard would go home to the hunter's wife while the hunter would go to look for deer. The hunter agreed, and the buzzard became a man and went home to the hunter's wife, who received him as her husband, while the hunter became a buzzard and flew off over the mountain to locate the deer. After staying some time with the woman, who thought always it was her real husband, the buzzard excused himself, saying he must go again to look for game or they would have nothing to eat. He came to the place where he had first met the hunter, and found him already there, still in buzzard form, awaiting him. He asked the hunter what success he had had, and the hunter replied that he had found several deer over the ridge, as the buzzard had said. Then the buzzard restored the hunter to human shape, and became himself a buzzard again and flew away. The hunter went where he had seen the deer and killed several, and from that time he never returned empty-handed from the woods.

THE RED MAN AND
THE UKTENA

Two brothers went hunting together, and when they came to a good camping place in the mountains they made a fire, and while one gathered bark to put up a shelter the other started up the creek to look for a deer. Soon he heard a noise on the top of the ridge as if two animals were fighting. He hurried through the bushes to see what it might be, and when he came to the spot he found a great uktena coiled around a man and choking him to death. The man was fighting for his life, and called out to the hunter: "Help me, nephew; he is your enemy as well as mine." The hunter took good aim, and, drawing the arrow to the head, sent it through the body of the uktena, so that the blood spouted from the hole. The snake loosed its coils with a snapping noise, and went tumbling down the ridge into the valley, tearing up the earth like a water spout as it rolled.

The stranger stood up, and it was the Asga'ya Gi'gagei, the Red Man of the Lightning. He said to the hunter: "You have helped me, and now I will reward you, and give you a medicine so that you can always find game." They waited until it was dark, and then went down the ridge to where the dead uktena had rolled, but by this time the birds and insects had eaten the body and only the bones were left. In one place were flashes of light coming up from the ground, and on digging here, just under the surface, the Red Man found a scale of the uktena. Next he went over to a tree that had been struck by lightning, and gathering a handful of splinters he made a fire and burned the uktena scale to a coal. He wrapped this in a piece of deerskin and gave it to the hunter, saying: "As long as you keep this you can always kill game." Then he told the hunter that when he went back to camp he must hang up the medicine on a tree outside, because it was very strong and dangerous. He told him also that when he went into the cabin he would find his brother lying inside nearly dead on account of the presence of the uktena's scale, but he must take a small piece of cane, which the Red Man gave him, and scrape a little of it into water and give it to his brother to drink and he would be well again. Then the Red Man was gone, and the hunter could not see where he went. He returned to camp alone, and found his brother very sick, but soon cured him with the medicine from the cane, and that day and the next, and every day after, he found game whenever he went for it.

THE SNAKE BOY

There was a boy who used to go bird hunting every day, and all the birds he brought home he gave to his grandmother, who was very fond of him. This made the rest of the family jealous, and they treated him in such fashion that at last one day he told his grandmother he would leave them all, but that she must not grieve for him. Next morning he refused to eat any breakfast, but went off hungry to the woods and was gone all day. In the evening he returned, bringing with him a pair of deer horns, and went directly to the hothouse (âsi), where his grandmother was waiting for him. He told the old woman he must be alone that night, so she got up and went into the house where the others were.

At early daybreak she came again to the hothouse and looked in, and there she saw an immense uktena that filled the âsi, with horns on its head, but still with two human legs instead of a snake tail. It was all that was left of her boy. He spoke to her and told her to leave him, and she went away again from the door. When the sun was well up, the uktena began slowly to crawl out, but it was full noon before it was all out of the âsi. It made a terrible hissing noise as it came out, and all the people ran from it. It crawled on through the settlement, leaving a broad trail in the ground behind it, until it came to a deep bend in the river, where it plunged in and went under the water.

The grandmother grieved much for her boy, until the others of the family got angry and told her that as she thought -so much of him she ought to go and stay with him. So she left them and went along the trail made by the uktena to the river and walked directly into the water and disappeared. Once after that a man fishing near the place saw her sitting on a large rock in the river, looking just as she had always looked, but as soon as she caught sight of him she jumped into the water and was gone.

THE SNAKE MAN

Two hunters, both for some reason under a tabu against the meat of a squirrel or turkey, had gone into the woods together. When evening came they found a good camping place and lighted a fire to prepare their supper. One of them had killed several squirrels during the day, and now got ready to broil them over the fire. His companion warned him that if he broke the tabu and ate squirrel meat he would become a snake, but the other laughed and said that was only a conjurer's story. He went on with his preparation, and when the squirrels were roasted made his supper of them and then lay down beside the fire to sleep.

Late that night his companion was aroused by groaning, and on looking around he found the other lying on the ground rolling and twisting in agony, and with the lower part of his body already changed to the body and tail of a large water snake. The man was still able to speak and called loudly for help, but his companion could do nothing, but only sit by and try to comfort him while he watched the arms sink into the body and the skin take on a scaly change that mounted gradually toward the neck, until at last even the head was a serpent's head and the great snake crawled away from the fire and down the bank into the river.

THE RATTLESNAKE'S VENGEANCE

One day in the old times when we could still talk with other creatures, while some children were playing about the house, their mother inside heard them scream. Running out she found that a rattlesnake had crawled from the grass, and taking up a stick she killed it. The father was out hunting in the mountains, and that evening when coming home after dark through the gap he heard a strange wailing sound. Looking about he found that he had come into the midst of a whole company of rattlesnakes, which all had their mouths open and seemed to be crying. He asked them the reason of their trouble, and they told him that his own wife had that day killed their chief, the Yellow Rattlesnake, and they were just now about to send the Black Rattlesnake to take revenge.

The hunter said he was very sorry, but they told him that if he spoke the truth he must be ready to make satisfaction and give his wife as a sacrifice for the life of their chief. Not knowing what might happen otherwise, he consented. They then told him that the Black Rattlesnake would go home with him and coil up just outside the door in the dark. He must go inside, where he would find his wife awaiting him, and ask her to get him a drink of fresh water from the spring. That was all.

He went home and knew that the Black Rattlesnake was following. It was night when he arrived and very dark, but he found his wife waiting with his supper ready. He sat down and asked for a drink of water. She handed him a gourd full from the jar, but he said he wanted it fresh from the spring, so she took a bowl and went out of the door. The next moment he heard a cry, and going out he found that the Black Rattlesnake had bitten her and that she was already dying. He stayed with her until she was dead, when the Black Rattlesnake came out from the grass again and said his tribe was now satisfied. He then taught the hunter a prayer song, and said, "When you meet any of us hereafter sing this song and we will not hurt you; but if by accident one of us should bite one of your people then sing this song over him and he will recover." And the Cherokee have kept the song to this day.

THE BULLFROG LOVER

A young man courted a girl, who liked him well enough, but her mother was so much opposed to him that she would not let him come near the house. At last he made a trumpet from the handle of a gourd and hid himself after night near the spring until the old woman came down for water. While she was dipping up the water he put the trumpet to his lips and grumbled out in a deep voice like a bullfrog's:

> *The faultfinder will die,*
> *The faultfinder will die.*

The woman thought it a witch bullfrog, and was so frightened that she dropped her dipper and ran back to the house to tell the people They all agreed that it was a warning to her to stop interfering with her daughter's affairs, so she gave her consent, and thus the young man won his wife.

There is another story of a girl who, every day when she went down to the spring for water, heard a voice singing, Kunu nu tutsahyesi, Kunu nu tutsahyesi, "A bullfrog will marry you, A bullfrog will marry you." She wondered much until one day when she came down she saw sitting on a stone by the spring a bullfrog, which suddenly took the form of a young man and asked her to marry him. She consented and took him back with her to the house. But although he had the shape of a man there was a queer bullfrog look about his face, so that the girl's family hated him and at last persuaded her to send him away. She told him and he went away, but when they next went down to the spring they heard a voice: Stetsi tuya husi, Stetsi tuya husi, "Your daughter will die, Your daughter will die," and so it happened soon after.

As some tell it, the lover was a tadpole, who took on human shape, retaining only his tadpole mouth. To conceal it he constantly refused to eat with the family, but stood with his back to the fire and his face screwed up, pretending that he had a toothache. At last his wife grew suspicious and turning him suddenly around to the firelight, exposed the tadpole mouth, at which they all ridiculed him so much that he left the house forever.

THE KATYDID'S WARNING

Two hunters camping in the woods were preparing supper one night when a Katydid began singing near them. One of them said sneeringly, "Ku! It sings and don't know that it will die before the season ends." The Katydid answered: "Ku! Niwi (onomatope); O, so you say; but you need not boast. You will die before tomorrow night." The next day they were surprised by the enemy and the hunter who had sneered at the Katydid was killed.

THE NEST OF
THE TLA'NUWA

On the north bank of Little Tennessee river, in a bend below the mouth of Citico creek, in Blount county, Tennessee, is a high cliff hanging over the water, and about halfway up the face of the rock is a cave with two openings. The rock projects outward above the cave, so that the mouth can not be seen from above, and it seems impossible to reach the cave either from above or below. There are white streaks in the rock from the cave down to the water. The Cherokee call it Tla'nuwâ'i, "the place of the Tla'nuwa," or great mythic hawk.

In the old time, away back soon after the creation, a pair of Tla'nuwas had their nest in this cave. The streaks in the rock were made by the droppings from the nest. They were immense birds, larger than any that live now, and very strong and savage. They were forever flying up and down the river, and used to come into the settlements and carry off dogs and even young children playing near the houses. No one could reach the nest to kill them, and when the people tried to shoot them the arrows only glanced off and were seized and carried away in the talons of the Tla'nuwas.

At last the people went to a great medicine man, who promised to help them. Some were afraid that if he failed to kill the Tla'nuwas they would take revenge on the people, but the medicine man said he could fix that. He made a long rope of linn bark, just as the Cherokee still do, with loops in it for his feet, and had the people let him down from the top of the cliff at a time when he knew that the old birds were away. When he came opposite the mouth of the cave he still could not reach it, because the rock above hung over, so he swung himself backward and forward several times until the rope swung near enough for him to pull himself into the cave with a hooked stick that he carried, which he managed to fasten in some bushes growing at the entrance. In the nest he found four young ones, and on the floor of the cave were the bones of all sorts of animals that had been carried there by the hawks. He pulled the young ones out of the nest and threw them over the cliff into the deep water below, where a great Uktena serpent that lived there finished them. Just then he saw the two old ones coming, and had hardly time to climb up again to the top of the rock before they reached the nest.

When they found the nest empty they were furious, and circled round and round in the air until they saw the snake put up its head from the water. Then they darted straight downward, and while one seized the snake in his talons and flew far up in the sky with it, his mate struck at it and bit off piece after piece until nothing was left. They were so high up that when the pieces fell they made holes in the rock, which are still to be seen there, at the place which we call "Where the Tla'nuwa cut it up," opposite the mouth of Citico. Then the two Tla'nuwas circled up and up until they went out of sight, and they have never been seen since.

THE HUNTER IN THE DAKWA

In the old days there was a great fish called the Dakwa, which lived in Tennessee river where Toco creek comes in at Dakwa'i, the "Dakwa place," above the mouth of Tellico, and which was so large that it could easily swallow a man. Once a canoe filled with warriors was crossing over from the town to the other side of the river, when the Dakwa suddenly rose up under the boat and threw them all into the air. As they came down it swallowed one with a single snap of its jaws and dived with him to the bottom of the river. As soon as the hunter came to his senses he found that he had not been hurt, but it was so hot and close inside the Dakwa that he was nearly smothered. As he groped around in the dark his hand struck a lot of mussel shells which the fish had swallowed, and taking one of these for a knife he began to cut his way out, until soon the fish grew uneasy at the scraping inside his stomach and came up to the top of the water for air. He kept on cutting until the fish was in such pain that it swam this way and that across the stream and thrashed the water into foam with its tail. Finally the hole was so large that he could look out and saw that the Dakwa was now resting in shallow water near the shore. Reaching up he climbed out from the side of the fish, moving very carefully so that the Dakwa would not know it, and then waded to shore and got back to the settlement, but the juices in the stomach of the great fish had scalded all the hair from his head and he was bald ever after.

THE BRIDE FROM THE SOUTH

The North went traveling, and after going far and meeting many different tribes he finally fell in love with the daughter of the South and wanted to marry her. The girl was willing, but her parents objected and said, "Ever since you came the weather has been cold, and if you stay here we may all freeze to death." The North pleaded hard, and said that if they would let him have their daughter he would take her back to his own country, so at last they consented. They were married and he took his bride to his own country, and when she arrived there she found the people all living in ice houses.

The next day, when the sun rose, the houses began to leak, and as it climbed higher they began to melt, and it grew warmer and warmer, until finally the people came to the young husband and told him he must send his wife home again, or the weather would get so warm that the whole settlement would be melted. He loved his wife and so held out as long as he could, but as the sun grew hotter the people were more urgent, and at last he had to send her home to her parents.

The people said that as she had been born in the South, and nourished all her life upon food that grew in the same climate, her whole nature was warm and unfit for the North.

THE ICE MAN

Once when the people were burning the woods in the fall the blaze set fire to a poplar tree, which continued to burn until the fire went down into the roots and burned a great hole in the ground. It burned and burned, and the hole grew constantly larger, until the people became frightened and were afraid it would burn the whole world. They tried to put out the fire, but it had gone too deep, and they did not know what to do.

At last some one said there was a man living in a house of ice far in the north who could put out the fire, so messengers were sent, and after traveling a long distance they came to the ice house and found the Ice Man at home. He was a little fellow with long hair hanging down to the ground in two plaits. The messengers told him their errand and he at once said, "O yes, I can help you," and began to unplait his hair. When it was all unbraided he took it up in one hand and struck it once across his other hand, and the messengers felt a wind blow against their cheeks. A second time he struck his hair across his hand, and a light rain began to fall. The third time he struck his hair across his open hand there was sleet mixed with the raindrops, and when he struck the fourth time great hailstones fell upon the ground, as if they had come out from the ends of his hair. "Go back now," said the Ice Man, "and I shall be there to-morrow." So the messengers returned to their people, whom they found still gathered helplessly about the great burning pit.

The next day while they were all watching about the fire there came a wind from the north, and they were afraid, for they knew that it came from the Ice Man. But the wind only made the fire blaze up higher. Then a light rain began to fall, but the drops seemed only to make the fire hotter. Then the shower turned to a heavy rain, with sleet and hail that killed the blaze and made clouds of smoke and steam rise from the red coals. The people fled to their homes for shelter, and the storm rose to a whirlwind that drove the rain into every burning crevice and piled great hailstones over the embers, until the fire was dead and even the smoke ceased. When at last it was all over and the people returned they found a lake where the burning pit had been, and from below the water came a sound as of embers still crackling.

THE UNDERGROUND
PANTHERS

A hunter was in the woods one day in winter when suddenly he saw a panther coming toward him and at once prepared to defend himself. The panther continued to approach, and the hunter was just about to shoot when the animal spoke, and at once it seemed to the man as if there was no difference between them, and they were both of the same nature. The panther asked him where he was going, and the man said that he was looking for a deer. "Well," said the panther, "we are getting ready for a Green-corn dance, and there are seven of us out after a buck, so we may as well hunt together."

The hunter agreed and they went on together. They started up one deer and another, but the panther made no sign, and said only, "Those are too small; we want something better." So the hunter did not shoot, and they went on. They started up another deer, a larger one, and the panther sprang upon it and tore its throat, and finally killed it after a hard struggle. The hunter got out his knife to skin it, but the panther said the skin was too much torn to be used and they must try again. They started up another large deer, and this the panther killed without trouble, and then, wrapping his tail around it, threw it across his back. "Now, come to our townhouse," he said to the hunter.

The panther led the way, carrying the captured deer upon his back, up a little stream branch until they came to the head spring, when it seemed as if a door opened in the side of the hill and they went in. Now the hunter found himself in front of a large townhouse, with the finest detsanun li he had ever seen, and the trees around were green, and the air was warm, as in summer. There was a great company there getting ready for the dance, and they were all panthers, but somehow it all seemed natural to the hunter. After a while the others who had been out came in with the deer they had taken, and the dance began. The hunter danced several rounds, and then said it was growing late and he must be getting home. So the panthers opened the door and he went out, and at once found himself alone in the woods again, and it was winter and very cold, with snow on the ground and on all the trees. When he reached the settlement he found a party just starting out to search for him. They asked him where he had been so long, and he told them the story, and then he found that he had been in the panther townhouse several days instead of only a very short time, as he had thought.

He died within seven days after his return, because he had already begun to take on the panther nature, and so could not live again with men. If he had stayed with the panthers he would have lived.

THE HAUNTED WHIRLPOOL

At the mouth of Suck creek, on the Tennessee, about 8 miles below Chattanooga, is a series of dangerous whirlpools, known as "The Suck," and noted among the Cherokee as the place where Untsaiyi, the gambler, lived long ago (see the story). They call it Untiguhi, "Pot-in-the-water," on account of the appearance of the surging, tumbling water, suggesting a boiling pot. They assert that in the old times the whirlpools were intermittent in character, and the canoemen attempting to pass the spot used to hug the bank, keeping constantly on the alert for signs of a coming eruption, and when they saw the water begin to revolve more rapidly would stop and wait until it became quiet again before attempting to proceed.

It happened once that two men, going down the river in a canoe, as they came near this place saw the water circling rapidly ahead of them. They pulled up to the bank to wait until it became smooth again, but the whirlpool seemed to approach with wider and wider circles, until they were drawn into the vortex. They were thrown out of the canoe and carried down under the water, where one man was seized by a great fish and was never seen again. The other was taken round and round down to the very lowest center of the whirlpool, when another circle caught him and bore him outward and upward until he was finally thrown up again to the surface and floated out into the shallow water, whence he made his escape to shore. He told afterwards that when he reached the narrowest circle of the maelstrom the water seemed to open below him and he could look down as through the roof beams of a house, and there on the bottom of the river he had seen a great company of people, who looked up and beckoned to him to join them, but as they put up their hands to seize him the swift current caught him and took him out of their reach.

www.sophenebooks.com

SOPHENE

www.ingramcontent.com/pod-product-compliance
Lightning Source LLC
Chambersburg PA
CBHW020656260626
47157CB00008B/3058